# CANARIES
## DYANNE ASIMOW

**⚏ BURROW BOOKS**

ISBN: 978-0-9859522-1-1

Cover illustration: Gina Rutmanis
Book design: Mackie Osborne

This is a work of fiction. Names, characters, places, and incidents are
either products of the author's imagination or, if real, are used fictitiously.

Published by Burrow Books • Los Angeles, California

Acknowledgements

A nod to Gilda Frantz
who was there when the journey began.
And then, cheering those first baby steps—
Anne Marie Martin Cappellino, Katy Parks Wilson,
Britta Lee Shaine, Julia Eisenman.
Along the way, buoying me with enthusiasm
and thoughtful critiques —
Janet Sarbanes, Stephen Foreman, Albert Chimedza,
Lindsay Maracotta, Rich Ferguson, Ted Humphrey,
Andrew Loschert, Marianne Dougherty, Gwendolyn Irby,
Karen K. Ford, Sid Stebel, Olivia Negron, Jackie Jaffe,
the Bad Girls Book Club, and Ronda Gómez-Quiñones.
Gratitude always for my sister, Andrea Asimow,
whose patience in reading, commenting and
re-reading keeps me from falling off the edge.

For my parents – Esther and Nate Asimow
— who introduced me to Death Valley.

For my children
– Raphael Simon and Jesse Simon
— who allowed me to share it.

# 1. Linda's voice

She, meaning I, but I'm calling her she — Linda — is not prepared to be the subject of a novel. She is not prepared to be Linda, but Linda will have to do. A neutral name. More dignified than Debbie or Tiffany, less formal than Jane or Ann; not the name she would have given herself — that name would have been Simone, back when she was sixteen, longing to be a French bohemian with full red lips and jet-black hair and a wild, passionate heart. For now, a simple Linda Gregory will suffice.

She lives in Los Angeles and suffers from an ailment no one perceives except her therapist.

"There's something wrong with your voice."

Linda's throat tightens. "You mean the way I said, 'Hello?'"

Words edge out, ambivalent, put-upon. She does not want to discuss her voice, although she thinks it's strange her therapist brought it up, because only yesterday, at her six-year-old son's soccer game, she was cheering wildly, but Sam didn't hear her, and later he asked why she hadn't been rooting for his team like all the other parents.

Doctor Faith Raven, IAAP, PhD in Psychology, Jungian Analyst, also a mother and a widow, stands up from behind her desk to look more closely at her eleven o'clock.

What does she see?

Dr. Raven doesn't see what you or I would see — an attractive thirty-five year old woman reluctantly named Linda framed in the doorway, her clean brown hair hanging straight and shiny, her dark brows un-plucked, her evenly proportioned weight shifting from one leg to the other; the baggy shorts, the sandals and skimpy tee-shirt not enough

1

to shield her from this scrutiny. We wouldn't know what brought her to the therapist's office, or that she's recalling her son's skeptical look when she told him the other parents' voices were so loud they overpowered hers, but we would notice the defensive smile, the curve of her tanned legs, the casual reveal of a bra strap as she shrugs her shoulders. The thin 18K gold wedding band.

Dr. Raven sees none of this. She concentrates on an agitated aura of colors, licks of red and orange choking Linda's neck.

"You should have it checked out," the therapist says. "I have a sense of these things."

An eye for pain. Drawn to it like the thirsty to water.

Linda sits on the overstuffed chair with matching footstool, both are upholstered in a floral motif. She slouches slightly, placing her feet on chintz maroon canna lillies. In this spot, each week, using skills she once employed as an English major, she attempts to define her story, locating archetypes and symbols in the details of her everyday life. She attempts to understand the paralysis that set in when she started to write this novel.

Faith gestures for her to proceed.

It suits Linda to call her therapist Faith, rather than Dr. Raven. Faith never went to medical school, and there is nothing doctor-like about her. The older woman dresses in soft rayon and twists her graying hair into a lopsided bun restrained by ebony chopsticks. Her office in the spring is full of tulips and daffodils. It's not neglected in summer, fall and winter, when it's replete with the seasonal bounty of the therapist's much-indulged garden, but Linda hasn't been seeing her that long.

She dodges the issue of voice, and dives into last night's dream.

"There was a great sucking sound from the vacuum cleaner. Then it began spitting. Dust spewed everywhere. My husband paid no attention. I tackled the canister — by now it was vibrating, and making a loud grinding noise, nails stuck in gears. I had to empty the bag — a task usually done by Ace-1, a weekly cleaning crew, the all-lesbian: 'WE TAKE LONGER AND DO IT BETTER.'"

She pauses. "Vacuum could be a play on words. Vacuum. Nothingness." She fiddles with her wedding ring. "Cleaning a vacuum." She looks at Faith. "Kind of what I do here, isn't it?"

Dr. Raven doesn't give her usual concurring nod. She seems only to be listening to the quality of Linda's vocal cords.

Linda holds up her hands. A surrender. "I can explain. At fifteen, I forced my voice into a lower register, so I'd sound like a real actress."

It worked, for a while. She'd won first prize in a Southern California regional speech and drama competition with her rendition of Kate in Taming Of The Shrew. But pushing the character's throaty sauciness had irritated Linda's vocal apparatus; she'd developed callus-like nodules and had been sent to the Children's Hospital outpatient clinic for breathing lessons.

"Not to worry," she reassures Faith, her voice contradicting with its lack of conviction.

A darkened room. A cold raised platform. A woman in white, placing her hand on Linda's abdomen, instructing her how to breathe. From the diaphragm. Not the chest. The diaphragm. In and out. Concentrate. Focus. How had it been that all of Linda's friends knew how to breathe, that even ignoramuses knew how to inhale and exhale without damaging themselves, but that she had to be taught?

3

"I never got the hang of breathing right. It's no big deal. I don't have the kind of life where I need to project."

She means she's not an actress. She gave that up by the time she was a sophomore in college. Nor is she a politician. Nor a motivational speaker. She's not a Drill Sergeant. She's not even a Soccer Mom who cheers loudly at her son's game.

Is she defined by what she's not?

Faith hears injury in the soft tones of explanation. The orange and the red swirl violently around the slender neck. If Linda were her daughter, she'd take her straight to an acupuncturist. But Linda is not her daughter. Faith has two grown children; the daughter has not spoken to her in three years.

"A voice expresses more than just a voice."

Faith is unwilling to drop the subject.

Nor should she. Voice resonates. In life. In a novel.

Linda's voice, for instance. What is the language, the tone, the shape? How many options are open to us, and how do we decide which one to select? Where do we locate the difference between a literary voice and a literal voice?

The sound Faith hears is breathy, a near-whisper, not evident on these written pages. Men appreciate the breathiness, the lucid thoughts ending hesitantly in question marks rather than exclamation points, echoes of Marilyn Monroe on sound waves listing towards their groin. There is something anachronistic about it, like foot-binding or whale-bone corsets.

Although the breathiness garners compliments, and a degree of flattering attention, the therapist is right, Linda admits on the way home. Her voice is wounded.

Worse.

"No voice at all. No story to tell. Or, if a story exists, no authority to claim it." She checks her rear-view mirror. There is no reflection. She adjusts the mirror. "Because we all have some kind of story, don't we?"

Perhaps not. Perhaps narrative doesn't exist, except in the telling. Perhaps Linda doesn't exist.

Once, when she was first married, she'd gone for three days without speaking to her husband. She'd nodded and smiled and cooked and written in her journals. Daniel had been quite content with the sound of his own opinions reflected back in those unobtrusive nods. She finally broke the silence because it terrified her. It terrified her that she could get used to it and never speak again.

A flash of yellow, a canary, crazed with freedom, careens in front of the car. She slams on the brakes. The bird disappears.

Linda's hand circles her throat.

## 2. Breath

This is a quote from Yoga, the Iyengar Way:

"Breath consists of the gross element of air and prana, the life force pervading the universe. Prana is the communicating link between the human organism and the cosmos. As it consists of energy, strong warnings are given against the practice of breathing without supervision, and before a student is ready."

What danger are we being cautioned against? What conjunction of inhalation and exhalation unleashes perilous anarchies of current? Into what vortex can a single breath plunge us?

Linda doesn't know. She hasn't read the book yet. She doesn't think about prana.

There are people in Linda's life, and her therapist may be among them, who confuse prana with self-expression, people who automatically assume creativity is good — the affirmation of life expressed through daily blogs, and holiday centerpieces erected out of pinecones and sparkle glue.

Even without reading The Iyengar Way, Linda knows better. She is a self-effacing person. The cosmos is not a personal mirror reflecting back her inner being. She behaves as if her survival depends on avoiding the vortex. She ought not breathe without supervision. Which presents a problem. Like the rest of us, she needs oxygen to exist; she compromises with shallow sips of air that barely disturb her lungs.

It's late. Sam is asleep. Her husband reads The Adventures of Augie March, the first book in the 'A's on Time Magazine's list of the 100 best English language novels, his latest mental-improvement project, displacing the New York Times crossword puzzle. He intends to read them all, ending with Wide Saragossa Sea. Daniel is the publisher of an online entertainment guide, a career he actually likes. "Why shouldn't I? People love to be entertained." He is successful, although not quite enough to satisfy his expectations. His body molds comfortably to the modular foam couch, a 70s retro piece in purple they found in a warehouse sale downtown.

After observing him a few moments, Linda asks, "Do you breathe from the diaphragm?"

Daniel, tall and lean, with thick, curly, salt and pepper hair, tangled locks meant for finger-running and Tchaikovsky competitions, for brilliance and seduction, this Daniel, her husband of eleven years, gets down on the hardwood floor, its planks of white oak scuffed because their 'no-shoes in the house' rule never gained traction, lies flat, and breathes. His stomach rises and falls. He consumes air as if he's entitled. He is heedless of the danger of prana.

"How'd I do?" He sits up, proud of himself, proud of his facile diaphragm.

"I'm going to take singing lessons."

Disbelief.

She can't carry a tune. No one in her family can carry a tune. When they get together for the holidays, and join in sing-alongs, they sound like seals barking off the Channel Islands. Worse, because seals are supposed to sound like seals.

"My therapist thinks–"

"Your therapist. I should've known."

Daniel can't bear Dr. Raven. He is convinced that the therapist, who he never has met, is against him. He takes

Linda's therapy personally.

"It has nothing to do with you," Linda protests, those occasions when he insists on discussing it, usually after dinner parties where he has assessed other men as leading lives more perfect than his own. "Why can't you see that?"

"We're married!" he invariably counters. "So, it has everything to do with me."

Situated in her own subjective state, Linda pays no heed to the impact of therapy on the institution of marriage. Nor does she consider Daniel's fear of losing her. It doesn't occur to her. She's not going anywhere.

"The teacher's name is Rosie." She says it almost tenderly. What a friendly, supportive name. She wishes she'd thought of it for herself.

She'd seen the notice posted on a bulletin board outside of Amoeba Records, where she'd gone to pick up the U2 remix for Daniel who felt that the rave reviews it had garnered reflected well on him, for being such a loyal fan. Amidst the profusion of ads for drum sets and amplifiers and roommates who would tolerate cats and cigarettes and loud noise at all hours, there had been a simple rose-colored card. "Voice lessons for the beginner. Rosie." And the phone number.

Linda read it twice.

Voice lessons.

Why not?

Deal with the issue directly.

Before she lost courage, she called.

"Hi, I'm Rosie. I'm out, but I check messages compulsively, so please leave one."

Linda imagined a large-bosomed opera singer pausing in the midst of a difficult aria, checking for messages. She did not imagine Rosie, in a short peach uniform, sashaying from table to table at Diner Joe's, waiting on customers and advising them not to skip Joe's famous gravy. She did not imagine Rosie on her break, using a cell phone next to the kitchen where reception was half-way decent, dodging the other servers as they balanced plates of steaming chicken pot pie and mashed potatoes while she hit voicemail, expecting — always — that one message which would change her life.

'Hello," Linda's whispery voice had begun. "I saw your notice. I hope you can help me."

Linda touches Daniel's arm. "Rosie. It's a nice name, isn't it?"

Daniel shrugs. It is unfathomable why his wife would spend time and money on a voice impossible to train, when she won't even take tennis lessons. Daniel's priorities are in place. Work, family, recreation. He is trying to combine family and recreation. If Linda took tennis lessons, they could spend time together on the courts. Long easy rallies on Sunday mornings. Wednesday night doubles. When Sam was older, they'd include him. Healthy competition clears the air. If Linda took tennis lessons, life would be easier.

"Daniel?"

He sighs, as if to signify, whatever is coming, it isn't good.

What she wants to ask is why he married her.

A pointless question. No response will quell the uneasiness that sent her to Faith Raven in the first place – turning thirty-five without a POV, blank pages remaining blank — and, since she's asked before, she knows. Wishing she'd touch his crotch instead of interrogating him, he'd reply that back in college, she'd not only been smart, but she'd had a soft sexy voice that kept him awake at nights, and that all the boys had crushes on her, and why wouldn't he have wanted to marry her?

She doesn't ask. Instead, she curls up next to him on the floor.

"Could you breathe again. I want to listen."

Relieved, he indulges her.

Linda positions her ear on Daniel's chest, and listens carefully to the air going in and out, each breath accompanied by the beat of his steady reassuring heart, and she feels safe.

# 3. The voice lesson

Dr. Raven is energetic about exploring voice imagery with Linda. She has covered a small table with bright yellow oilcloth on which she's placed a glob of red clay. She wants Linda to envision the nodules along her vocal cords, and then sculpt them.

As Linda mashes her hands into the moist terra cotta, poking and pinching and rolling, she wishes Sam were with her, it would be more fun. More like pre-school, although now he's in kindergarten. He likes to play with clay. She does not. She compels reluctant fingers to cooperate, to shape and reshape until small round heads are formed, with tongues that stick out at her, and goatees like Rasputin, and horns of the devil.

Faith approves.

Linda lines up the little clay monsters. She pretends they are inside her throat, jostling to block any emerging sound. Her muscles constrict.

Dr. Raven checks them out. "Who are these nodules?"

No answer.

"What are the names of your nodules?"

The therapist sounds as if she's talking to a four-year-old. Linda stiffens, then responds in kind. A childish tone. "This is Daddy, that's Uncle Jack, here's my so-called best friend in 3rd grade..." The edge of irony bounces off Dr. Raven who believes, because she must, that this process helps Linda connect with her shadow, the dark interior where unpleasant impulses lurk, that part of the psyche to which Jungians are so drawn. She believes they are making headway.

Does Dr. Raven, Faith, stop to consider that the notion

of a shadow self took root in sedate, homogenous Switzerland, in the mind of a privileged man who lived by a beautiful lake, who never had to deal with drive-bys or homeless panhandlers or internet trolling? Linda doesn't ask. Nor does she divulge that in a nation of guns and road rage and economic disparity, of a boozing, addicted, terrified populace careening out of control, restraint, even repression of one's own dark-side, makes a certain sense. Linda does not pay two hundred and twenty-five dollars an hour on a sliding scale to discuss social concepts.

Together, the therapist and the client gaze at the clay heads.

"What about Daniel? Is he one of the nodules?" asks Faith.

Linda reflects. "Maybe." She pokes an unfinished, misshapen ball. "Maybe not."

Blaming Daniel would turn her into a victim. She's not a victim. She married Daniel of her own volition.

She stares at the lump.

"Do you want to smash them?" asks Faith.

"No." She picks up the misshapen lump and carefully smooths it out. She makes an egg. Her palms are crusted with terra cotta. "They can't help who they are."

Faith presses against her eyelids. It seems her retina is unduly sensitive to the slashes of red energy cleaving to Linda's throat. Her deceased husband used to brag to his colleagues about his wife's ability to see auras. The colleagues, all Jungians, were sympathetic to the metaphysical; even so, they had difficulty believing she actually saw what she claimed.

When Faith opens her eyes, the aura dissipates. "I wish you'd see someone. An acupuncturist."

"I'm going to see a voice teacher," Linda replies. She

envisions herself by an open window overlooking the palms and the acacias, liquid soprano notes trebling from her vocal cords in a tone so pure the birds pause in flight to listen.

And the Voice Teacher? What is she doing the morning of the lesson? She goes to Clean Coin Launderland, the biggest laundromat in the neighborhood. Rosie doesn't own a washing machine or a dishwasher or a garbage disposal or a microwave or a garage door clicker. She has nothing against modern conveniences or the energy they waste; she just doesn't have the money, and she is too stubborn to kowtow in front of her withholding mother who doesn't have much to give, anyway. Her Joe's Diner tips go to music, massage and shoes, in that order. Rosie loves massages. She is a connoisseur. She has been kneaded and pushed and stroked and walked on; her limbs have been twisted and stretched; her skin has been oiled and hosed and beaten with switches of fresh eucalyptus. She has been massaged by all sorts of men and women, including an old coot in Desert Hot Springs who used one gnarled hand to stroke her and the other to stroke himself. ("How could you not know!" asked a friend. "My eyes were closed," she explained. "I didn't realize until I heard him panting.")

The Launderland's motto is "why wait." The dryer obediently finishes with her clothes in record time. Next to her, a Latina woman folding sheets admires her turquoise scoop-necked blouse.

"You know why the earth came to make turquoise?" asks the woman without waiting for an answer. "She was jealous of the sky." Touching the fabric, "Preciosa."

So that Sam won't interrupt her lesson, Linda has negotiated for him to stay with a friend.

She picks Sterling Silver roses from the garden and arranges them in a metal vase. She rearranges them. She wishes she knew the Japanese art of Ikebana so she could arrange them more beautifully. The desire for beauty overcomes her. She remembers her mother's description of a great-aunt's house. "She made the house sing". By that, her mother meant the furniture was polished until it gleamed, even the tops of picture frames were dusted, and sheets were tucked so tightly coins could bounce on the surface. But to Linda it suggests a house filled with harmony, and in the center — the perfectly chosen flower in the perfectly chosen vase.

There is a knock on the door.

Rosie is not wearing the turquoise blouse. She gave it to the Latina woman at Clean Coin Launderland. In exchange, the woman handed Rosie a candle in a tall glass with a decal of Saint Mary Magdalene on it, assuring her if she lights the candle, she will get her heart's desire. The blouse is a small price to pay, reckons Rosie.

She is dressed in green. Dark green suede ankle boots, long pea green very tight skirt with slits, chartreuse ribbed tee shirt, an olive tote. The greens compliment her copper hair.

"You're Rosie?"

Not what Linda was expecting.

"I wasn't sure about putting my ad up at Amoeba's. But then I thought, if I can't trust my instincts to weed out the nutcases...." Rosie stops, afraid she's insulted Linda.

Linda is not insulted, though she ponders the question as she leads her new teacher into the house and offers her something to drink. With only a phone call to go by, how can you tell if someone is a nutcase?

"Wow," says Rosie, as they enter the fully equipped

kitchen, "So Williams-Sonoma! You must really like to cook! I never have time for anything but ramen and three-minute eggs."

Linda wants to defend herself. But there's nothing to defend. She likes to cook.

Rosie accepts a bottle of water.

"Have you ever done any singing?"

Abruptly, Linda wants to call off the lesson. "No."

The sterling silver rose, which is actually lavender in color, ceases to matter. This can't possibly work out.

"Great. A clean slate. No bad habits. That's important."

Rosie slings her bag on the purple modular couch in the living room.

A clean slate. No bad habits. Linda feels better. A fresh slab of clay.

"So, what do you do?" asks Rosie.

Linda searches for an appropriate response. Is the singing teacher asking, how can she afford to live in a gracious Spanish house with hardwood floors and genuine early Californian tile, retro furniture, a view of palms and acacias, and a Subzero refrigerator that purifies water for ice cubes? Is she being pre-judged as an at-home wife, a dilettante filling her time with lessons?

She does not reveal that the house was purchased right before Sam was born when her husband shepherded the transformation of a popular entertainment guide into the digital world. E-tainment became number one in the heady atmosphere of social media just as traditional print was gasping for air. Nor does she explain that she'd earned her share of the down payment by editing technical journals, a career which bored her so much she was nauseous all the time and didn't even notice when it became morning sickness, so accustomed was she to regurgitating.

That's not what Rosie's asking.

"I'm writing or trying. I thought voice lessons might help me find my — you know — my voice. Explore it physically, then tackle narrative."

She's babbling.

Rosie nods, but her gray eyes are distant. Linda is the first person to respond to her business card, and she is uncertain about protocol. Her student hasn't asked for proof that Rosie can actually teach. Coughing politely, she interrupts Linda, and runs through her credentials, listing her vocal teachers, their training techniques, how long she studied with them. She invites Linda to hear her sing at the Ground Bean during open mic nights. Finally, she asks Linda what her goal is.

Linda drops the issue of narrative authority.

"Don't worry. I don't expect to sing arias from La Boheme."

Rosie shakes a finger. "Never limit yourself."

They need a comfortable place for Linda to sit, a place where Rosie can watch her mouth. The modular couch isn't right. Like two animals finding a nest, they circle pillows and ottomans and chairs, before settling at the dining room table.

"Let's begin."

Lesson One.

Relaxing the tongue.

# 4. Linda's tongue

There are many ways to think about a tongue.

Tongue-twisters.

Tongue-tied.

Silver-tongued.

The organ of speech.

The organ of taste.

A food shovel.

The tongue forms food particles into a bolus by cupping. The tongue's middle portion depresses while its anterior, posterior, and lateral portions elevate against the hard palate, the roof of the mouth. During the pharyngeal phase, pressure of the bolus against the anterior faucial arches triggers the swallow. Pharyngeal peristalsis carries the bolus through the pharynx to the top of the esophagus.

Then, there is the tongue Linda's Grandma bought from the butcher, which she boiled and sliced and served with mustard.

Tongues salted and hung to dry on the mantles of huge stone fireplaces in the Middle Ages.

Coated tongues, white with thrush, in the mouths of sick babies and AIDS patients.

An exotic stranger's tongue in Linda's mouth and elsewhere, licking, lapping, palpitating her to orgasm. So far, this hasn't happened.

When Rosie asks, "What do you think of when I say the word, tongue?" Linda can't answer.

Rosie sticks out her own tongue. It's pink and lively. Linda leans in close to see the genioglossus muscle, the superior longitudinal muscle, the three kinds of papillae on the surface. She examines the tongue's position when tense, and its position when relaxed.

She nods as Rosie explains the importance of the tongue in speech and in vocalizing. The importance of a relaxed tongue.

"Your turn," Rosie says.

Linda wiggles her tongue, curls the tip, pushes against her hard palate, then curls it under, touching the sublingual fold, inadvertently activating the salivary gland. Her mouth is awash in saliva. She worries that she will drool.

"Now relax it. Let it just flop," instructs Rosie.

A pause.

Linda needs to swallow. She can't. Rosie's scrutiny has inhibited the swallowing function. People have choked on their own saliva. Linda worries it might happen to her, right there in her dining room, in front of the brass samovar her husband's great-grandmother brought over from Poland, in front of Rosie, her new voice teacher who doesn't look like one.

The pause continues. Linda worries that she is boring Rosie.

Is Rosie bored? Do her thoughts wander to the candle with the picture of the saint who will grant her heart's desire? Not at all. She is excited by her responsibility as a teacher of voice. She sees Linda's delicate Adam's apple struggling. She wants to swallow for her but realizes that a teacher must let her pupil learn by doing.

"Take a deep breath," she recommends. "From the diaphragm."

At that, Linda almost spits up. Then gulps. She has swallowed. Pharyngeal peristalsis has accomplished its purpose.

Now she will relax her tongue.

It pokes one side of her cheek, then the other. It sits

rigid and unyielding in the center of her mouth. It is not responding to her instructions. She shrugs apologetically.

"Try this." Rosie fakes a yawn, lower mandible swiveling back and forth, silver fillings and a gold crown unabashed in the rear molars.

Linda is conscious of her own jaw locking tight.

Tongue. Lingua. Language. Native tongue. Mother tongue.

She tries again. She jams it as hard as she can against her lower teeth, then quickly releases. The tongue goes limp. She hesitates, then takes a breath, a small inconspicuous breath, not from the diaphragm. The tongue remains flaccid.

Now begins a unique experience in Linda's conscious life.

A succession of incomprehensible emotions wells up and spills out, crashing waves of sorrow and fury and manic joy, leaving her exposed and vulnerable. That's not all. Torrents of external sensation surge in. Nothing is there to stop it. Her tongue has been the watchdog, the fence, the gate, the Reichian armor protecting her from the world. No longer. Tears sting her eyes. Linda is stunned at the difference a relaxed tongue makes.

She stares with awe at Rosie.

Rosie checks the time on her cellphone. The lesson is over.

## 5. A nap

All week Linda practices. She clenches her tongue, and then relaxes it. Each time, she feels that wave of vulnerability. Daniel hasn't noticed, but Sam, his six-year-old eyes drawn to any deviation in her appearance, says, "How come you do that funny thing with your mouth?"

It's Sunday. Daniel leaves for the office to catch up on work.

Linda smiles and sticks her tongue out at Sam. He smiles back and sticks his tongue out. Their tongues wave at each other, like snakes in greeting.

"Mine's a rattler!" hisses Sam.

"Mine's a swan," replies Linda.

"A rattler can kill a swan," gloats her son.

"Not if it swims away." And she paddles through air all the way to the fridge, where she takes out a jar of peanut butter and glues the roof of Sam's mouth to the mid-section of his tongue. "Let's take a nap."

"I'm too old!"

"Well, I'm not."

Depleted by sensation, she needs a nap.

This shift in the posture of her tongue has had consequences. Without Cerberus at the gate, there is no filter. Linda has no organizational grid for the impact of sensations. They come at her with equal weight. Love for her son, irritation with 'gotcha' pundits on cable, suspicion her husband would rather be at work than be with her.

A question. If we all stretch out for a nap — you the reader, Linda, and I — if we close our eyes at the same time, allowing half-formulated thoughts to drift in and out of our consciousness — will the story proceed? How much guidance does the author have to provide?

Linda would like to abandon her narrative. Or else allow us to structure it for her.

Like a sleepwalker she wanders the house, past the silver rose about to lose its petals, a still life, 'nature morte', a meditation on the ephemeral, until she finds herself in the spare bedroom. A place without distractions. Small and tidy. It smells of guest soap and clean towels instead of her marriage.

She places pillows under her knees, a throw over her body. The door remains open in case Sam needs her. Without thinking whether she wants to or not, she places her hand between her legs.

The first time she masturbated to orgasm was the summer she spent in New York, a few months after she'd lost her virginity. She decided to teach herself how to climax since it had failed to happen during sex. In a hot stuffy room at the economically priced, parental approved YWCA, while she was supposed to be attending City College summer school, she spread her legs and rubbed her clit until she came. Having done it once, she did it again and again and again, sitting on the john, taking a shower, under the sheets at night when she thought her roommates were sleeping, or, unable to stop herself, even when she knew they weren't. An orgy, all summer long.

Linda's fingers lightly press down. She experiments; tightening her tongue at the same time she tightens her inner thighs and buttocks, then slackening. She can't get a rhythm going. Her muscles don't cooperate. The two tongues stay out of sync.

Letting it slide, she closes her eyes, fingers limp inside her underpants.

Can a rattlesnake kill a swan? drowsily she wonders.

In England, lives a species called the Mute Swan. Drawn by the name, Linda went to the trouble of looking it up. There is a popular misconception that Mute Swans pair for life and that a bird will pine to death when its partner dies. In fact, some birds have as many as four mates in a lifetime, and there are cases where a mate is actually 'divorced' in favor of a new one.

Once, earlier in their marriage, before Sam was born, Daniel returned, flushed and nervous, from a tennis game. He confessed that he'd had a wild fling in the back of a van with his tennis partner, a woman they'd known for years. Linda sensed he was as turned-on by his guilt as he'd been by the actual sex. In a self-exculpatory speech, he described what had transpired. The vivid details assaulted Linda. Bruised by too much knowledge, she wrenched a promise from him — so guilt-ridden, he would have agreed to anything — that he would never confess again. At the time, what troubled her as much as Daniel's betrayal of marital trust was the high decibel level of his excitement. She recognized that he had traversed into some dark murky region of passion, and she had no idea how to follow him there. But since that one transgression, he never has philandered, to use an old-fashioned word.

True, there are unexpected dinner meetings with old-time TV stars for an article that has yet to be posted in print. The occasional Sunday at work. Apologetic cell phone departures to the back deck during the evening news. But if he is wandering, there have been no ripples to disturb their marriage, and she knows Daniel well enough to know that he could not conduct an affair without ripples.

A nap eludes Linda.

# 6. Rosie sings

To Linda's surprise, Daniel is quite enthusiastic about hearing the voice teacher sing at open mic night. He looks forward to an excursion in NoHo, a section of North Hollywood that fancies itself SoHo West, although its sullen boulevards, burdened with names like Burbank and Oxnard and Lankershim, continue to be known for their car dealerships and cut-rate mattress shops, and the uninitiated are mystified by the explosion of 99-seat theaters, stylish condos, the proliferation of cafes catering to a new kind of palate.

"It'll be different," he says. "When's the last time we went somewhere different?"

Linda appreciates Daniel's energy; she appreciates that he isn't sulking about her voice lessons. She puts on a tight black dress and spends extra time applying her make-up. From the bottom of the jewelry box she removes a flaming fire opal pendant with matching earrings that Daniel gave her on their first anniversary. Sam says she looks like someone else's mom; Daniel says she should dress that way more often.

The Ground Bean is a former appliance store, converted into a coffee house by the presence of second-hand furniture and a glaze of polyurethane on the ochre-splotched cement floor. A plywood platform with a sound system squats at one end. Patchouli is in the air.

Linda and Daniel evoke stares. Too dressed. The wrong age. Unlike the regulars barely out of their teens, they don't scuffle over to familiar tables or sprawl across the lumpy couch, playing games on iPhones while unlit cigarettes hang from their lips. Our couple's outsider status is even more obvious when the two actually study a menu penned in looping red marker on a white board over the espresso machine. Linda opts for dark roast organic fair-trade decaf. Daniel goes for lava java, full throttle.

Neither is cognizant of a small buzz hovering about their presence. Like a swarm of Africanized honey-bees, the buzz expands– psst... he's a talent scout... psst... they're agents... psst... she's a small books publisher... psst...psst....

Rosie, perched on a stool, hair tucked under a 40s hat with a black net veil, sips tea with honey. She hears the air vibrate, and then a whisper: "Isn't he from Warner Records?!"

She spins around.

Daniel stands there. In a sea of juvenile posturing, he is the only one who could be from Warner Records. Sophisticated, yet casual, sublimely attuned to the crowd, his gaze sweeps the room, honed, she imagines, by nights in clubs pursuing undiscovered talent. So certain is Rosie that he is canvassing new venues, searching the Ground Bean for his next indie hit, she would've bet her entire month of tips on it.

In fact, he's just looking for a table while Linda is off to the restroom.

An unfortunate circumstance. If Linda were standing next to him, she would have seen Rosie and waved. Rosie not only would have realized that Daniel was married to her new pupil, but, also, that he was not from Warner Records. However, due to a casual plot point, if a full bladder can be considered casual, Daniel is alone, and Rosie, with a brief prayer to Saint Mary Magdalene of the Laundromat candle, wills him to turn towards her.

There is a choice here. He could stay focused on the

task — finding a table. Or he could turn. Not a difficult choice. When he turns, she catches his eye, his dark, possibly roving, soulful eye, and she lifts her veil and flashes him her most brilliant smile. He smiles back.

"He saw me!" she announces excitedly to the keyboard player.

The keyboard player, immediately depressed that he'll never be good enough to be signed to a label, feigns indifference. "I can't think of a single person who was discovered at The Ground Bean."

"Well, think again!" Rosie swings her leg, crossed at the knee, sling-back heel suspended carelessly from the tip of her toe.

She's committed to an extraordinary destiny as a chanteuse, the Edith Piaf of her generation, not as tragic but equally famous. There are windswept evenings when she drives her beat-up Corolla straight to the top of Mulholland; she gets out, poised above the splash of glittering Valley lights, and, unconcerned who might witness her, she spreads her arms in a big welcome to her future fans.

Rosie darts another look at Daniel, making his way to an empty table, juggling two coffee mugs and a slice of chocolate decadence. He manages another tilt of his head in acknowledgment of her regard.

Tonight will be her night.

Preoccupied with latrinalia, latrine wall scrawl — 'GOD IS LOVE, BUT SATAN DOES THAT THING YOU REALLY LIKE WITH HIS TONGUE' — Linda leaves the genderless restroom. Her admiration for public toilet graffiti extends from the outlandish sexual proposals misspelled in glitter lipstick to the erudite insights etched into enamel paint. What Linda admires is the utter confidence conveyed by the graffiti writers. Their appropriation of private/public space. Their conviction that under the right circumstances, people will read whatever is in front of them.

Heads turn as she makes her way towards Daniel.

The speculation heats up. Had she once been a dancer in a Gap ad?

Linda, immersed in connecting graffiti and the rise of the novel, is oblivious. She doesn't see Daniel. She doesn't catch his appraisal, the way he's checking her out, his unconscious comparison to the woman whose smile caught his eye. Linda mulls whether the invention of the printing press led to a new, anonymous audience, the novel as graffiti, spilling out of the presses into the hands of unknown readers. Of course, the young people at the Ground Bean, with their primate thumbs racing across smart phones, wouldn't care. Yes, the glut of social media is the newest iteration, but for her, pixels don't have the visceral potency of sitting on a toilet deciphering messages, or the intimacy of a book on a lap.

Loud screeches from the sound system inaugurate open mic night. The emcee, a woman with an inked Celtic triangle on her forearm, gestures Rosie up to the platform. Rosie takes a moment to adjust her hat, the veil.

Linda finds Daniel and grabs his shoulder, excited.

"That's her! That's my singing teacher!"

She has no idea that while she was on the toilet, Daniel and Rosie made eye contact, that because she spent a few minutes longer than she should have reading verbiage on the stall door, her life is about to be changed. Because she doesn't know, she is unconcerned, and fails to note his reaction.

Which is what?

Regret? A poignant pang at bidding adieu to the fleeting fantasy warming his search for an empty table? Daniel's a prudent man, and he's not about to have a quickie with his wife's voice teacher, even if their eyes did lock across a crowded room. On the other hand, to be fair, he might not have had such a fantasy. A good-looking heterosexual male who doesn't wear a wedding ring must receive a lot of come-hither looks from attractive women. Perhaps his departures during the evening news, the phone calls he takes outside of Linda's hearing, are due to his efforts to say 'no' to all the women under the misapprehension that any response to their flirting means 'yes.' Since the debacle with his tennis partner, Daniel is acutely aware of the perils of a one-night stand.

As if to prove this point, he leans in close to Linda and tells her she looks great, "better than all the bohos in NoHo!"

The fire in the opal pendant flickers brighter.

They share the slice of chocolate decadence with the easy absence of boundaries that comes from years of marriage. She licks the fork, and her lips, then reaches over with the corner of her napkin to wipe off a chocolate crumb from the edge of his mouth. He manages to sneak in a brief nibble on her finger, and pays no attention to Rosie, now adjusting a bra strap. We can conclude he smiled at her because she smiled at him, and there was nothing more to it.

For him. Not for Rosie.

Rosie is dreaming about a record contract.

The lights shine directly in her eyes, obscuring faces in the audience, making it impossible to recognize Linda, who she's only seen for one lesson, and who she isn't expecting anyway. Thanking the emcee for the intro, she lifts up the microphone and launches into her own rendition of Billie Holiday's "The Very Thought of You."

Rosie's voice melts into the air. The low tones reach inside the stomach and squeeze the guts. The high notes seize the heart.

What had been true minutes earlier is no longer true.

Daniel sinks inside the song, and never ever wants to leave.

# 7. Bedtime stories

"She was incredible!" Linda enthuses to her therapist. "Her voice was smoky; it was incandescent." She is unaccustomed to expressing such ardor. "I'd give anything to be able to sing like that."

Dr. Raven frowns.

Linda reacts. "I don't mean I'd give my right arm, or my first born, but she's like... she's like a canary. She opens her mouth and music pours out and the room glows and, well, it's a gift. That's all."

A pause as we examine Dr. Raven's frown.

Years ago, Faith's daughter also had said, "I wish I could sing like that." The girl had been extolling the virtues of a caterwauling maniac with hateful eyes and skin scored by obscene tattoos, a false idol who polluted the world with offensive videos as well as equally offensive posters plastered all over the once sweetly rainbow-and-unicorn decorated bedroom. Faith loathed the music. She loathed everything the performer represented. Her mistake was to convey as much, and her daughter, furious at having her taste questioned, slammed the door on their relationship. Faith would have retracted the words, reconciled, but before she found a suitable opportunity, her husband's heart condition worsened. In the years since his funeral, the daughter graduated college and moved to North Carolina where she works for pharmaceuticals in R&D. They have not spoken since, not really.

The frown is not the judgment Linda thinks it is.

Dr. Raven, unexpectedly reminded of her double loss, and still unable to forgive that caterwauling maniac who she blames, becomes teary at the limitations of human nature, especially her own. Rather than the tissue she keeps in a box for clients, she takes out an embroidered handkerchief and dabs her eyes.

Though Linda fails to understand why she has upset her therapist, she apologizes.

"No, no. It's not you." Faith crumples the handkerchief. "I'm sure the singing teacher has a lovely voice." She smooths out the handkerchief and folds it into squares. She regains her professional mien. "But for our next session, I want you to write a story in which you locate your own lovely voice."

Linda's tongue stiffens, wedging itself against her teeth. "I can't! I'm stuck." Her tongue is chained to vocabulary, sentence structure. Mired when words don't come. Arms fold tight against her chest. "Singing is very different from writing a story."

Faith doesn't respond. Linda struggles to describe what she means.

Song is emotion, rhythm, a melody coursing through one's body, forging synapses of non-verbal sensation. No novel, not even Joyce's Ulysses, though he tried, can do that.

Words fall short. She gives up. Her tone is as arid as the Mojave Desert. "Whatever voice I might locate, I'll never hit the high notes or stay in tune."

Faith says, merely, "Give the story a try."

That night, Daniel isn't around. Business dinner going late. Linda doesn't think much about it. She's used to it, just as she's accustomed to Daniel's exposure to beautiful women — actresses, starlets, anyone angling for a mention in his E-tainment website. Celebrities are a part of their lives, even at Sam's school and the local farmers' market. She doesn't worry, nor do we, that he might have palmed

30

Linda's rose-colored card with Rosie's phone number printed on it before he left for work in the morning.

It's Sam's bedtime. She lies next to him on his bunk bed, lights dimmed. He wants her to tell him his favorite bedtime story — the exploits of a little boy named Sam.

Instead, Linda begins telling him about the Queen who lost her voice.

"I don't want to hear that one."

"You've never heard it before."

"I know how it goes."

Linda raises herself on an elbow to look at him. "You do?"

"Sure. She wakes up in the middle of the night after a bad dream and she tries to scream and nothing comes out."

"What happened?" Linda asks.

"Her voice got scared and ran away."

He is a living miracle, this young son of hers whose brain never stops. She marvels at his lips, perfectly shaped, with just a hint of babyhood pout.

"How come it got scared?"

Sam shrugs. "Maybe it said a bad word and didn't want to get punished."

"Does she go look for it?"

"Of course, dumb-bell. You always have to go look for the thing that runs away. Otherwise it's not a story."

"Okay. So she sneaks out of the castle and disguises herself so no one will know she's the queen. A little frog follows her. He knows where the voice is hiding."

"What's the little frog's name?" Sam's eyes begin to close.

"His name is Sam."

A satisfied smile creeps over his face. He's asleep before Sam, the frog, can show the Queen where the voice is hiding.

Linda hurries to her computer. She opens a new file and titles it, "The Queen Who Lost Her Voice." She replaces 'Lost' with 'Found.' She writes quickly, trying to trick her subconscious.

It doesn't work. Just as the frog is prepared to disclose the location of the missing voice, Linda's mind shuts down. Like it always does. She waits. She plays with Spell-Check, Thesaurus. She changes a noun — wart — to 'excrescence,' then to 'bulge,' then back to 'wart.' She does a frog search on Yahoo! and discovers that amphibians see only in black and white.

She remains stymied.

A new file. "Fuck!" she types across the pristine page. "Fuck, fuck, fuck!"

She deletes the file.

Does she try to distract herself by checking her e-mail? Who corresponds with her anyway? We've been remiss in not having established friends, especially Stephanie, her best friend since Junior High. She and Stephanie e-mail each other frequently, even if only to share funny snippets or links to oddball sites. Ordinarily, Linda likes the ritual of sitting down, composing thoughts, sending them off, waiting for a reply, dispatching and receiving notes like one of Jane Austin's heroines, which is why she refuses to text.

Tonight, unable to put herself inside the little frog's black and white head, unable to locate her own unique voice, she procrastinates by going to 'comments' on Let's Write, a support site designed to propel the notion that anyone can do it. The first comment that pops up — brilliant surreal his Buddha heart shining through — causes her to flee all commentary.

She stares at the screensaver. She does not e-mail. She does not surf the net. She does not message or chat or seek refuge in Instagram or Tik Tok or any other social media. She wishes she had a voice like Rosie, and that she didn't need a frog to show the way.

## 8. Bel canto

Rosie does not suspect that Daniel is Linda's husband. She looked for him after open mic was over, but he had gone. She managed to swallow her disappointment, grateful the keyboard player refrained from gloating. Nonetheless, small clouds of gloom hovered. When he phones the next day, and suggests they meet for drinks, the clouds evaporate, the sun comes out, the sky is blue, and she is convinced Saint Mary Magdalene of the Laundromat candle was listening after all.

They sit in a lacerated booth in an East Hollywood bar, the jukebox wailing Tejano border songs. Daniel has chosen the bar judiciously, to avoid being seen by anyone he might know. Secrecy is unlike him. He only has strayed once during his marriage, with a tennis partner, confessed immediately, and was told by Linda not to do it again — he never was certain if she meant confess, or have extra-marital sex, but in either case, it was irrelevant. An affair didn't cross his mind. Until now.

Tonight, Rosie's hair is not hidden under a hat. Its copper sheen lights up her corner of the booth. Daniel can't take his eyes off her. She fiddles with her purse strap, nervous about making the right moves toward fame and fortune.

As soon as her hot lemon water and his vodka martini arrive, Daniel blurts out that Rosie's singing makes him feel like an awkward adolescent with an uncontrollable dick, that he is mortified by the intensity of her power over him.

She smiles, delighted.

He fishes out the olive from his martini. "The problem is, I'm married," he mumbles, chewing the olive, as if that will muffle the starkness of the situation.

"I'm not looking for a relationship," Rosie responds, using her chest voice, the one that goes straight to the groin.

He can't stand it. "Your voice should be declared a deadly weapon." He takes her hand, touching the smooth long fingers, and he fails to notice Linda's friend, Stephanie, recently obsessed with salsa dancing, coming in with her salsero.

"Can you guess what I do want?" Rosie inquires, slyly.

"What? Anything. I'll get it for you. I'm besotted. I'm like those diva fans in the opera house who can't stop shouting bravo, bravo, bravo."

"A recording contract."

He lets go of her hand and gulps down his martini.

"Well, if you think my voice is so great…"

He gestures for another.

"I don't get it. Why'd you want to have drinks with me?" She lifts her eyes and they are swimming with tears.

Daniel's balls ache.

"I'd be perfect for Warner Records."

"Huh?"

"Warner Records. I'd be perfect."

"I have no doubt. Absolutely."

Her face is radiant once again. "Then you'll help me!"

"How?"

"Obviously, you have a good ear, or you wouldn't be where you are. They listen to you, don't they?"

Daniel stares into his second martini. The silvery liquid beckons him to drown.

If he tells her he has nothing to do with Warner Records, she might never see him again. If he pretends to see what he can do, he's no more than an outright cad.

He is not accustomed to such an unappealing array of

options. He's the good guy

"Don't they?" repeats Rosie.

He smiles sadly. "I'd like to think everyone listens to me, Rosie. But if I did, I'd be a fool."

# 9. The anointed

If Linda could sing like Rosie, would it make a difference?

In gospel churches, they say the spirit of the Lord is in the anointed voice. The anointed voice has so much power, they say, it can bring down walls and raze civilizations.

Linda is certain she is not among the anointed.

## 10. Breakfast blues

Early in the morning, before the marine layer has burned off, before trucks blast their way up the quiet street, before she is quite conscious, Linda drifts to Daniel's side of the bed, her fingers reaching for the warm imprint left by his body, a caress in absentia. This is the time of day when she is most appreciative of Daniel. Like a domestic Napoleon, he marshals the forces: bagels into the toaster, juice on the table, Sam out of pajamas and into school clothes, backpack stuffed with lunch, a favorite action figure, an extra pair of socks to replace those mysteriously missing in the course of a day, signed parent/teacher notes if needed.

Occasionally, this morning, for instance, Daniel is inspired to make pancakes. Linda hears Sam's excited voice crying, "Higher, Dad, higher!"

The image of Daniel flipping flapjacks high into the air never fails to win her heart. She fell in love with him the night he made a porcini mushroom omelet. While expertly tossing it, he had turned to see her reaction. At that moment, the eggs somersaulted over the pan and landed on the floor. Fortunately, he'd placed newspaper down to catch stray flakes of onionskin and garlic peel. Linda didn't mind a little newsprint. With a bottle of red wine, she and Daniel sat cross-legged on the floor and ingested the literate omelet and each other and by the time they were done, she knew he'd be the one she'd marry.

The space on his side of the bed is already cold. A faint patchouli stain in the air teases her nose. She opens her eyes.

"Hey," she greets Sam and Daniel in the kitchen. She is wrapped in a kimono, her hair tousled, and her demeanor still soft with sleep. She heads for the coffee. "Did you go back to the Ground Bean last night?"

Daniel holds very still. "Why?"

Mug in hand, she leans against the counter. "I thought I smelled Rosie's voice." She smiles, but it's true. That voice is in the air — smoky, incandescent, rife with musk of patchouli.

"I told you, a business dinner!" He abruptly turns to Sam. "Come on, kidlet, time for school."

"I haven't finished my pancake!"

"Take it with you, then."

After the sound of the car engine fades away, there is silence. Some mornings, she feels swathed in a cozy peaceful calm. Not today. Today the silence is loud. It thuds across the room, heavy, ominous. She barricades herself with the coffee mug. She pushes at it with the newspaper, the real one, not a digital one. Smoothing out Daniel's folded sections, stretching the paper to its full awkward size, she reads the editorials and finds her horoscope, as if other people's opinions and predictions can provide her with the answers to all her unasked questions.

"Forget about it," she mutters to the horoscope, brushing off omens of astrological disruption. "Why make a mountain out of a molehill?"

In all probability, her own dress had picked up the scent during Rosie's performance, and in dusky reverberations from the music, it echoed from the bedroom closet. Patchouli was like that. Katmandu to Ibiza, patchouli melodies drifting by, an aromatic map for the hippies of old to follow.

Linda sighs. She doesn't have a map. She has no idea where she's going next.

Do authors ever just give up in the middle? The narrative strangled at the very moment our heroine faces the wall we instinctively expect her to climb?

"Dear reader, sorry, no catharsis. No resolution. The end of the line."

That would be too cruel. And unnecessary. A simple adjustment can make a difference, a new character, a shift in plot. Or conversely, a wild, reckless throw of the dice, chance determining outcome. No. Not that. Linda isn't ready for that kind of risk. Not today. Not yet.

We'll start with simple. See where that goes. This morning, instead of feeling sorry for herself, instead of staring blankly at her computer mulling over frogs, or worrying about voice, or turning molehills into mountains, she smells gas. A leak from the expensive professional grade stove they'd bought two years ago.

She recalls how canaries once were used to detect toxic gases in coal-mines, toxic gases which had no smell. How many canaries died in order to save the lives of miners? she wonders while she phones the Gas Company. The Gas Company promises to send someone over.

The last time she called them, Sam was three. Three years ago. She and Daniel had an old stove they'd found on Craig's List when she was pregnant, and they were exchanging their hip but inappropriate rental for a child-friendly one. The stove worked most of the time, but the day she'd called, the burners had ceased to function. Matches didn't do the trick. She would have waited for Daniel to come home, except she'd promised Sam she'd make butterscotch pudding, his favorite, and let him lick the pot.

It was a hot afternoon. One of those hot, dry, Santa Ana days, the heat sweeping in from the Mojave. The kind of day that detective stories employ to foreshadow mayhem and violence. Sam and a pre-school friend were outside, clothes off, playing with a garden hose. Lugging stools and a plastic storage crate, they climbed to the top of a stone terrace and used the crate as a stage.

"Come see our water show," commanded Sam, spraying bright yellow daisies and fuchsia bougainvillea, chortling as he doused the pretend audience. In loud sweet voices the two sang in time to the fluid music of a rubber hose twirling giant circles of water in the air.

The gas man was adjusting the pilot when the two slippery preschoolers ran through, making puddles, skidding on the tile, landing on their bare bottoms and squealing with delight.

"Not that many folks let their kids go naked anymore," commented the gasman to Linda.

She'd looked at the boys, glistening cherubs, their small penises unprotected from the gaze of this potentially prurient gasman. "Well, it's hot," she said, as neutrally as possible, wondering if he were going to lecture her that she was not a good mother.

The man faced her. "I'm a nudist myself," he announced. "I guess you wouldn't know that, seeing as I have my clothes on."

Linda wasn't sure how to respond. He hadn't fixed the pilot light yet.

"I belong to a nudist club out in the desert." He moved in closer to her.

She tried not to be obvious as she backed away. "That's interesting."

"I like working naked."

He was a big, burly man. The image wasn't appealing.

"Like you said, it's hot. So why don't the two of us be au naturel, the way god intended?"

God did not intend her to be au naturel with this man. The hair on her neck stood up. An involuntary response to creepiness. She wanted him out of the house as quickly as possible. She also did not want to antagonize him, possibly put herself in danger, or worse, the kids in danger.

"What do you think is wrong with the stove?" she asked.

He had not been deflected by her question. But he fiddled with the pilot light, testing each burner, one by one, slowly, as if to give her time to make up her mind. When all four burners were blazing, he turned to her.

"I didn't think you were uptight." His eyes locked on her breasts.

"My husband's coming home any minute. He wouldn't appreciate it."

That didn't faze him. He picked one of Sam's trucks off the floor and began to straighten out the bent axle.

"Look," Linda said, angered by her vulnerability. "I have nothing against it. But it's not something I believe in per se. I don't think the Gas Company does, either."

He wasn't an idiot. His jaw tightened. He knew a threat when he heard it. He put Sam's truck down. He stepped toward her.

How could she have been so stupid? She was a woman, alone with two young children. What kind of protection did she have? She was wearing flimsy flip-flops. No sharp pins held up her hair. The chopping knives were too far for her to reach if he chose to pin her against the wall. Her fingers balled up into fists.

"Thanks a lot for fixing my stove," she uttered as neutrally as possible under the circumstances.

He moved in closer. "What'd you say?"

Her nails drew blood in the balled-up fists. "Thank you for fixing the stove."

It was her voice that had saved her.

"You sound like the actress, what's her name, the one with the raspy voice. I always liked her." With that, he'd picked up his toolbox and left.

Daniel came home that night to the remains of butterscotch pudding and the news that the stove was unreliable and they had to sell it immediately. When they were in bed, she told him what happened. His reassurance became love-making, in the midst of which they both got the giggles, picturing the nudist gasman.

'Hairy butt' became their giggle-prompter for months after.

This time, three years later, it occurs to her that by calling the Gas Company she is inviting trouble. Maybe the same man will come and he'll remember her and the situation won't end as well. But still, there is the odor. No ignoring it. She is relieved when the Gas Company sends a woman, big and burly also, with a pleasant countenance and a no-nonsense manner.

"Good to learn how to fix these things yourself, you know. No need to be frightened of gas, as long as you're careful. Of course, some people aren't, and they blow their heads off."

The Gas Company woman adjusts the sensor.

Linda thanks her.

"I'm getting too old for this job, especially checking the meters," the woman confides. "I weigh too much. My bones ache. I can't outrun the dogs anymore."

All day, Linda thinks about being too old to outrun the dogs.

Daniel comes home in time for dinner. She has made coq au vin in the perfectly regulated oven.

"What's the occasion?" he wants to know.

She moves close to him and inhales. He smells like Daniel. Her Daniel. She buries her face in his chest. His arms automatically slide around her. Sam comes bouncing in. He wants to be in the middle. The three of them stand there, swaying together, a family.

# 11. Squeaking by

Dr. Raven does not appreciate our last chapter's adjustment.

"Patchouli. Gas leaks. You seem to be very focused on odors and smells today."

Linda tenses. In those sessions when she refers to sound, timbre, pitch, the therapist doesn't question it. When her ruminating relates to voice, especially a voice choked by hostile-colored auras and in need of healing, the therapist is full of encouraging nods. There are no such nods now. The lack of them indicates implicit judgment.

Why is this? Does there exist a hierarchy of value regarding metaphors? Has sound become more elevated than smell? Sight more elevated than touch? And where on the ladder do we find taste? Is Dr. Raven the Metaphor Police? These seem like legitimate questions, but Linda doesn't ask them. Instead, during a long pause, her shallow breath audible, she pursues them into the territory of synesthesia.

What if voices are scents? What if her reality is saturated by synesthesia, a cacophony of all her senses, none more important than another, one replacing the next? What then? Would Dr. Raven send her packing because of inferior metaphors? She begins cataloguing: If Rosie's voice is patchouli, then Daniel's is late autumn, sharp and crisp, and Sam's is the aroma of freshly baked bread. Faith's voice is definitely crushed mint. Linda's own voice–

"Are you avoiding?" prods the therapist.

Her train of thought interrupted before she pins down her own voice metaphor, Linda balks. Taciturn stubbornness elongates until she reminds herself that she's paying to be here.

She speaks. "By avoiding, do you mean talking about the scent of patchouli rather than the person who's wearing it? Or inventing the smell of gas to express how I feel about myself — a vague unpleasant odor, which, if not contained, will explode in everyone's face?"

Dr. Raven tilts her head, interested at last.

"Are you implying that I should connect the gasman, and my inability to protest what could've been an ugly sexual situation, to how I couldn't or wouldn't say anything to Daniel about his business dinner the other night?"

A slight satisfied smile indicates, yes, that's exactly what the therapist is implying.

"What if that's way off?" Linda is determined to erase the satisfaction, prove Faith wrong. "What if the reason I even thought of the gasman is because, well, yes, there could be this hint of doubt —if even that — about Daniel and where the patchouli came from — but what if it's something entirely different? What if the gasman represents sexual possibility and freedom? The guy had a gut, but he was lusty and unafraid to be naked. Maybe he never existed, and I made him up as an object of desire."

"So you desire the gasman?"

Linda shakes her head. "No."

"Do you desire Daniel?"

A long pause. Linda's eyes open wide as if there is not enough light available to see the answer.

No scent of patchouli when Rosie, all business, comes in for Linda's next lesson. Instead, a reassuring whiff of lavender. This time Linda does not fuss with floral arrangements or arrange a playdate for Sam. In fact, she considers it educational for him to watch the lesson.

When she puts out a candy bowl — a wedding gift from

a television network executive with their monogram etched into the Waterford crystal — Sam's arm darts out, ready to take a handful of chocolate mints.

"They're for the singing teacher."

"She gets all of them?" He is horrified.

"No, but they're not for right now. After the lesson, you can have one."

Rosie pays no attention to the mints. She doesn't glance around, so preoccupied is she with her lesson plan. So preoccupied, in fact, that she doesn't notice the framed family photos placed on end tables, including an especially nice one of Daniel and Sam taken on Father's Day, a clear cool day at the beach just after a game of frisbee, thus allowing the fantasy that has warmed her for the last few days to remain untarnished.

"You were wonderful the other night," says Linda.

"At the Ground Bean? I didn't see you."

"We had to leave right after your set, but you were wonderful."

Rosie doesn't mention that she met someone from Warner records, and he's going to help her get a contract.

"Today I want you to make a sound," she informs Linda.

"What kind of sound?"

"Any kind. Relax your tongue. Relax your throat. Let a sound emerge."

Linda tries to imagine a sound. She can't. She becomes short of breath. She leans against the wall, while Rosie waits, expectant.

Sam goes, "I can make a sound."

He roars like a lion. Rosie pats him on the head, but explains that it's his mother who needs to do it. Linda tells him to go outside and play, that he's inhibiting her.

"What's inhibiting?"

"Just go on!"

Sam leaves, grabbing a chocolate mint.

"Okay," Linda hyperventilates. "How hard can this be?"

She relaxes her tongue. She relaxes her throat. With Rosie's hand on her diaphragm, she takes a breath.

Lungs stretched with air, Linda readies for vocalization. She will make a sound. Any sound. An operatic high C, or an ohm, or a jubilant cry, or a mournful wail.

The sound she emits stuns her.

A squeak. A tiny mouse squeak. She's given it her all, and that's the extent of what she can do. Blood drains from her head. Dizziness overwhelms her. Unaware that she has turned paper white, she slumps to the floor.

When she comes to, Rosie is hovering with a glass of filtered water.

"Do you want me to call a doctor?"

A squeak is the most ignominious noise Linda can imagine. Hinges squeak. Rodents squeak. Rubber toys squeak. Frightened excitable women squeak.

"I can't believe I fainted," she says.

Rosie extends her hand and helps her up. They sit on the couch. Rosie worries her teaching technique is at fault; that somehow, she's responsible for Linda's fainting.

Linda shakes her head. "No, it's me. I could be one of those hysterical patients, the kind that Sigmund Freud used to treat — only instead of a paralyzed arm, I have a paralyzed vocal cord!"

Rosie smiles uncomfortably and looks away. This is beyond the field of her expertise. She shifts her gaze to the objects on the end table near the couch. Daniel's iPad is there. So is a plastic action figure. And, in an acrylic frame with exposed screws, a photo of Linda, Daniel, and Sam.

"I have a lot of work to do, don't you think?"

Linda's question distracts Rosie before she has a chance to really look at the photo. "How do you mean?"

"On myself. Something is very wrong here."

"Try visualizing." Rosie believes in visualization; it's a tool she employs in her reach towards stardom. She's glad she can make a concrete suggestion.

Linda likes the idea. She'll visualize; she'll send warm healing energy to her hysterically paralyzed larynx. "What do vocal cords look like?"

"Well, normal cords have smooth, white mucosal surfaces without any irregularities on the vibrating borders." Rosie is sure of herself. She's been studying. To be great, she needs to know everything there is to know about singing.

"I'm sure mine have irregularities all over them. My therapist is convinced I should see someone." Linda reconsiders Faith's opinion. Maybe she should follow the advice. If she had a clear picture of the inside of her throat, she could visualize correctly.

Rosie volunteers the name of a prominent throat surgeon. Dr. de Boer.

"He handles major opera stars. He's the best in Los Angeles. Even my singing teacher went to him."

Dr. de Boer.

Linda pays Rosie for her time.

"I guess I'll stop taking lessons until after I've seen the doctor."

Rosie stifles her dismay. She'd factored in the extra income she'd be earning and bought an extravagant pair of Christian Louboutin platform pumps for the next time she saw her Prince Charming from Warner Records. Now she's going to be short at the end of the month. She puts the money in her bag, which is on the floor right below the photo of Linda, Sam and Daniel.

She glances at the photo. She glances again. She picks it up and stares directly into Daniel's eyes.

"Is this your husband?" she asks.

The lavender in her voice crumbles into dust.

The local news does not report the burglary at a Los Feliz neighborhood pet store. This particular crime is too small to register on the same scale as brutal slashings, kidnappings, bombings, scandals. One stolen canary. Nothing else taken, not even the bird cage, which is worth far more than the bird. Still, it's a shock. When Linda goes into the pet store, ostensibly to pacify Sam's desire to look at puppies, the place is atwitter with worried employees and concerned customers and the local cop asking questions.

Sam has reluctantly accepted the fact that he isn't going to get a puppy. He's allowed only goldfish because his father is allergic to dog fur, cat hair, duck down, and angora. Linda exposes Sam to as many animals as possible to make up for the deficiencies of goldfish, which are not interactive pets under the best of circumstances, and, in Sam's case, they die with such regularity that he ceased burying them and flushes them down the toilet instead.

The last time this happened, Linda questioned his lack of sentiment.

"Goldilocks (the fish's name) thinks it's like a waterfall," he explained. "She likes it better than being in the ground."

Sam is a convenient excuse for Linda. The canaries are the real reason she has come. She needs vocal inspiration, and canaries are all throat and vocal organ and warble and whistle and purveyor of trills that carry quaint ambiguous names like Hollow Roll, Hollow Bell and Flute.

A fact about canaries: No two sing the same song, each composition is unique — a voiceprint.

The missing canary is a clear yellow German Roller.

Linda, who never shop-lifted, not even in middle school

when Stephanie was in her klepto phase, taking lipsticks from make-up counters and stuffing her bra with expensive panties, Linda nonetheless finds herself empathizing with the canary thief, the desire to steal a bird, to steal its song, that uncertain moment of should I/shouldn't I and then the succumbing to temptation. She'd never do it herself — or so she says — but she imagines a shadow — perhaps that of a mousy girl working in an anonymous cubicle, or an old lady living off food stamps and her dead husband's Social Security, or even a former debutante divorcée in altered circumstances — one of contemporary society's erased figures sneaking into the pet store in the dark of night when the birds are asleep. Heading for the yellow German Roller's cage, one hand full of a mixture of mashed egg and ground soybeans with raw sunflower seeds and poppy seeds and bee pollen. Waiting for the first trusting nibble, that first peck, then nabbing the bird with a fine linen cloth, and taking it home. The appropriation of a tiny feathered body vibrating with unadulterated joy of song.

Linda more than empathizes. She identifies.

The policeman comes up to her. "You know anything about this?"

It sounds like an accusation.

Is it?

Police are trained to read body gestures. Can he also read her mind? Did Linda's imagination give her away? The vivid recreation of the theft of the German Roller, down to the linen cloth, could have been a chapter in this book all by itself.

Caught in the imagined act.

She blushes guiltily and shakes her head.

His eyes linger on her.

Why the blush, if she's innocent?

I'm not a thief! Her brain denies the accusation, but she doesn't say it out loud.

To prove him wrong, forgetting her husband is allergic to feathers as well as dogs and cats and horses and rabbits, with a defiant toss of her hair she says, "I want to buy a canary."

"You picked the worst time," the saleswoman replies. "We need them all as evidence."

"You mean them boids are gonna sing like a canary?" jokes a customer.

Linda smiles broadly at the joke, too broadly, obviously forced. The saleswoman frowns and glances at the policeman. They both look at her. They think she did it. Linda is convinced. Criminals often return to the scene of the crime. She's read the mysteries, the thrillers. Unable to resist spying on the aftermath. That's how they get caught.

"We're leaving," she says to Sam.

"Mom, the puppy loves me!"

He sits on the floor next to a puppy cage, letting a six-week-old Beagle lick his finger.

"We'll come back."

Sam presses his cheek against the wire so the puppy can kiss him goodbye.

Before they reach the door, one of the canaries, a male variegated American Singer, puffs his feathers, and bursts into his song. The pet store becomes quiet. Even the cop listens, transfixed. The American Singer has a full melodious tone. He combines Flutes, Bells, and the sounds of water bubbling into a free-style lyrical medley. When the bird is finished, the humans in the pet store break into spontaneous applause.

The canary takes a bow and hops onto a different perch.

Linda wants to take a bow as well. She no longer frets

about the thief. She smiles a genuine smile at the cop. She waves good-bye to the saleswoman. She hugs Sam who hugs her back. The canary's solo has filled Linda with hope. Her caged voice will someday be free. She will sound like that.

Not exactly like that. Her own song. Her own voiceprint. She has made an appointment with Dr. de Boer.

## 13. Rosie's plan


This time it doesn't work. Rosie stands on Mulholland Drive, perched like Winged Victory over Studio City, her arms spread, her breasts thrust forward. While the wind whips up her skirt, she proclaims that she's the greatest singer of her generation. Nothing happens. No electrical currents run through her veins. No neon glow of future fame envelops her person. No responding affirmation from the Valley.

It's Daniel's fault.

Rosie paces the decomposed granite. She's due at Joe's Diner, but if she's this out of sorts, she will make zilch in tips. There's no point going until she's ready to beam brightly at Mr. Gus Santini and Miss Robin Luther, who'll be having sand dabs and Caesar Salad, no raw egg in the dressing, and who always tell her how much they enjoy her vivacious personality. If she's not vivacious, they'll take it personally. Not only won't they tip her, they might find another place for their weekly rendezvous. Rosie kicks a rock. It flies over the cliff. She hopes it lands on Daniel's head and knocks some sense into him.

What kind of sense is she after?

Rosie never has had an affair with a married man before. Not that she's slept with Daniel, but she's been considering it, and, although, right off the bat, he did admit to being married, it was a theoretical concept — a faceless wife who she'd never met — and any compunction she'd had about affairs with married men had been directed towards herself — it's the single woman who gets hurt. She knows this because of countless magazine articles, advice columns and anecdotes from girlfriends. She had factored in heartbreak, and decided it was worth the risk. But she hadn't anticipated that he was Linda's husband. He should've told her. He should have told her he was not at Warner Records, nowhere near Warner Records, that he'd come to the Ground Bean because his wife was Rosie's new student. He didn't lie, but he left out the details. He misled her.

She kicks another rock.

Why should she care so much, anyway? Linda isn't her student anymore. Which means Rosie won't be making the money she was counting on to pay off her credit card. It also means that if she sees Daniel again, and he's asked her to, he's begged her to, as a matter of fact, Linda wouldn't have to know about it. There won't be any lessons during which Rosie might accidentally betray such a secret liaison. That's right. Linda quit. Backed out of a commitment after discovering that all she could do was squeak.

Let's stop Rosie here. She isn't a mean person. She isn't a vengeful person. She has nothing personal against Linda, who she hardly knows. Nothing against her, except that she's married to the man who Rosie thought was going to make her famous. Let's give Rosie a second to absorb what she saw — Daniel who is not a record producer but a family man, the husband of her student and a loving father, all of which the photograph made clear.

It obviously was painful for her to see that. Will she take the time to ponder the meaning of family? The fragility of that nuclear unit? The delicate balance needed for its survival?

She paces the valley side of Mulholland, getting closer and closer to suicide gulch, aka Deadman's Curve, the point where cars have skidded off, or been pushed off, their rusted bodies covered by chaparral. She is too deep in thought to notice or care.

Daniel is not a record producer, he's the head of a successful on-line entertainment digest with millions of fol-
lowers, a fact that was immediately available when she
Googled him after that dismal last lesson with Linda. Why
hadn't she given up on the idea of him immediately?

It takes Rosie a moment to sort things out. We can wait.
Possibly, we think, she will be relieved not to sleep with him
now, thus sparing herself as well as Linda a lot of heartache. A lizard scurries away from her foot and down the
cliff before she can kick a third rock.

The moment comes and goes. A different set of calculations presents itself. It goes like this: Daniel has got to be
on first-name basis with everyone; that's part of his job.
Important people kiss up to him. They fast talk, cozy up,
pull out all the stops, badger and hound him to mention
their names or groups, their TV specials or their Netflix series or their music awards shows, and if and when he does,
they owe him. They owe him favors. Daniel probably has a
whole piggy bank full of uncollected favors. He easily could
use up a few of them. He could orchestrate a meeting for
her with anyone of those people. If he cared to. And if he
saw her again, he would.

Rosie lights up. She blows a kiss to the Valley. She calls
him at his office and tells him she can't wait to see him. She
has a song she wants to sing for him. It'll knock his socks
off. And maybe even, she pauses for emphasis, his pants.

Linda phones Dr. Raven to cancel this week's session.

"I have an appointment with Dr. de Boer. He's not an
acupuncturist; he's a throat specialist who treats opera
singers. I wanted you to know I took your suggestion se-
riously."

The news surprises Faith. Over the years, no matter

how good the counsel might be, her daughter never listened to her. And yet, from the moment she exclaimed that she would give anything to sing like Rosie and became, in Faith's mind, a surrogate for her alienated daughter, here was Linda, who actually took her direction. Proving once again that clients are not surrogates. Dr. Raven should have known better than to try to work out her own dismal daughter-mother relationship using Linda. She did know better. She just couldn't help it.

"You'll tell me what Dr. de Boer thinks the problem is, if he finds one, I mean."

"Of course!"

As far as Linda is concerned, the appointment is an extension of therapy, her two doctors, Raven and de Boer, consulting on the mystery of her vocal paralysis.

Origins unknown.

Is that important? Should we find a certified-hypnotherapist or a past lives specialist to help recover repressed memory? Or is that just a way to build specious suspense? Linda would tell us it is not necessary, her memory is fine, and she certainly does not want to write about it. There is no reason to doubt her when she says she never was raped or molested. No lascivious uncle or deranged neighbor traumatized her larynx, terrifying her into silence with the threat that, should she reveal anything, her parents would pay with their lives.

If not abuse, or PTSD, then what?

Did cultural expectations wrap around her neck and choke her until the voice became a whisper? Interrupted mid-sentence; credit for her suggestions appropriated by male colleagues; judged by decorum; hearing 'where's the smile?' one time too many; the drip, drip, drip of being treated as just slightly less than?

This is a direction Linda doesn't mind exploring.

Starting when she was a teenager, she read books on the topic of adolescent female self-esteem. She thrilled to Simone de Beauvoir whose frankness and existential rigor in The Second Sex, found on her parents' bookshelf next to Our Bodies, Ourselves, shaped her sense of self and her potential. She remembers quite clearly skipping over the descriptions of oppression that happened to women in adulthood, so confident she was that it wouldn't happen to her. Later, for one of her college psychology classes, she read a number of contemporary studies dissecting the psychological noose that tightens around a young woman after she reaches puberty, even in the post-Title IX era when it's recognized that girls can do math or play basketball if they're allowed. Linda accepted the validity of those studies, but, for herself, she saw no tightening. She still doesn't.

"I don't think I had a psychological noose around my neck at the onset of puberty," she insists to Daniel over creme brûlée that she made with Sam, who has eaten his portion and run off to finish building a Lego doghouse for his Lego dog. They are sitting on classic chrome and burnished leather stools at the charcoal slate counter in the kitchen. They could be a couple featured in Dwell magazine. "I raised my hand in class. I was never afraid to speak my mind. It wasn't like my parents put a muzzle on me."

She is looking for feedback.

"I wouldn't exactly call you frank with them." Daniel scrapes the bowl for the last of the creme brûlée, delicious, though not elegant.

"Well, no point in upsetting them about things they don't need to know."

Therapy, for instance.

She is quite aware of what their opinions about Dr. Raven would be. Therefore, why bother? Why allow her father to get all worked about his own fear that going to a shrink releases repressed emotions; opening a Pandora's box, they all come tumbling out, and there you are — buffeted by feelings you can't control. Then, her mother. Why give her mother another opportunity to judge? She wouldn't see the value of a therapist because what in god's name was there for Linda to talk to a therapist about? Healthy, married, with a wonderful husband and child, food in her mouth, a roof over her head — she should consider herself lucky, instead of wasting money. When Linda was growing up, her mother counseled her not to make an issue about small matters. Sensible advice, but what if life consists only of small matters, and by never making an issue, she did stifle her voice? Not a muzzle, but....

She puts the question to Daniel.

"What if some molehills ought to be mountains?"

Because he is not a mind reader, he does not follow her meaning.

"Maybe that's why my vocal cords are paralyzed. I never squawked and fussed over seemingly insignificant things."

"Linda, if you were to spend your days squawking and fussing over insignificant stuff it would not make your voice any louder, just a lot whinier."

"So you agree with my mother."

He pours himself more wine. "I don't think you have to yell to be heard."

She thinks back. "The truth is, I did argue with my parents. I argued about curfew. I argued about my hair. I argued about the existence of God."

She lost the argument over her hair. When she paraded into a cousin's wedding with her silky chestnut hair

chopped and bristling, peroxided into a disaffected plati-
num boasting inky roots, no mitigating sheen or highlights,
her mother wept and her father, unsettled by his wife's
unusual display of emotion, accused Linda of ruining the
bride's special day.

"You're a freak!" he charged. "Everyone's looking at
you instead of the bride. Does that make you happy?"

The words blistered Linda. He had crossed over a line.
She hurled her sixteen-year-old, Simone de Beauvoir en-
lightened self at him. "You have no right. It's my hair. Not
yours. I do not belong to you."

The very next day, her father, who never before in his life
had set foot in a beauty salon, stood there with his arms
folded until every strand of hair was forcibly restored to its
natural color, and re-styled from outrageous to pixie.

For the record, she won the argument about God, but it
didn't much matter.

Teenagers always fight about hair, Linda tells Daniel. As
a matter of fact, she now completely understands a parent's point of view. When Sam's baby curls were shorn the
week before he started pre-school, she wept. She hadn't
realized the sheer joy she'd derived from watching the gos-
samer strands fly up and catch the sunlight.

"Honestly, Daniel, I can't recall a single childhood ca-
lamity above and beyond the normal ones of falling into a
cactus or being stung by a bee or having my feelings hurt
by girls turning against me in fifth grade."

"Why don't you see what Dr. de Boer says, instead of
analyzing it to death."

He takes the plates to the sink, thus avoiding the dark
glance that Linda throws his way.

"What's on your sweater?" she asks. "It's full of lint."

Daniel raises his arm. Pink fur adheres to the black cotton knit.

She goes over and pulls some off. She rolls it between her fingers. "It's angora."

"Angora?"

"Yes, angora. Like the yarn. I thought you were allergic."

"To what?"

"To angora."

"I am. It must not be angora. Otherwise, I'd be sneezing, wouldn't I?"

She stares at him. She knows it is angora. She knows he is allergic.

A description of angora sex will evolve in a later chapter, but right now it is too soon for Linda to know about Daniel and Rosie. They scarcely know what's happening themselves. As for Daniel's disappearing allergy, that's a function of histamines. Suffice it to say, an afternoon with Rosie curtailed the production of stress-related histamines. They won't re-emerge until a sneezing bout much later in the evening, at which point Linda will think, "I told you so. Angora." But she won't say it out loud.

Dr. de Boer doesn't disappoint. He has a steel gray goatee, with small wire-rimmed glasses and a full head of hair, slicked back. He does not have a European accent, but Linda attributes one to him. She has him immigrating from post-war Belgium with parents who lost their banking fortune while barely escaping Nazi persecution.

Photos of singers — pop, opera, gospel, musicals, jazz — decorate a short white passageway leading to his examining room. "Thanks for saving my pipes," scrawled on one. "Couldn't hit high-C without you, Doc," on another.

Linda is too nervous to pay much attention. She fidgets as she arranges herself on the cold plastic casing of a sky-blue multi-sectored ENT chair. She repeats her history of

adolescent nodules and tries to articulate why it's important to visualize her vocal cords in dealing with her loss of
narrative voice. Dr. de Boer responds to nothing she says
except the name of Rosie's singing teacher.

"Oh, yes, Miss Sampson, mezzo-soprano. Unfortunate
woman. Throat cancer. Is she teaching now?"

Linda nods yes, as if personally acquainted.

"Well, let's take a look at you and see – " his eyes twinkle — "if there's anything to visualize." He readjusts the
position of the back of the chair and reaches for a small
angled mirror.

His voice is pleasant, well-modulated, relaxed. She
wonders if he's had to practice speaking that way.

De Boer wraps her tongue in gauze — like a mummy's
tongue — then firmly takes hold of it and pulls hard. With
his other hand, he holds the mirror against the back of her
palate. The twinkle disappears. His expression becoming
quite grave, he reaches for a flexible viewing tube.

"This may be a little painful," he warns.

He applies an anesthetic lubricant, and gently inserts a
tube down her throat. She represses the impulse to gag.
He puts his eye next to the lens.

His face is extraordinarily close to hers. She can see
the individual hairs of his goatee, the pores of his cheek,
the folds of his ear. He smells slightly disinfected, as if he's
prepped for surgery. She notices a small scar, white, the
shape of a crescent moon, not far from the corner of his
mouth.

Does he have a wife? she wonders. A small petite woman with long painted nails who cooks Waterzoi every New
Year, recreating smells of Brussels. Or is it Antwerp?

His face lifts away from hers. The tube slips out. He
hands her a glass of water. She sips gratefully.

"My dear, there is a very large tumor on your vocal cord." He shakes his head in disbelief. "I'm amazed you can speak at all."

# 15. The tumor

Tumor.

The mere mention generates apprehension. Not a word to brush away with easy reassurance. Not a word to use lightly.

Tumor. A malignancy. A growth. A protuberance. Polyp. Sarcoma. Cancerous. Death. There are no comfortable reassuring synonyms.

In the arousal of dread, Tumor has superseded Satan.

Evil. Sin. Polluted. We toss these words around loosely. They don't stop us in our tracks. They don't put us in touch with a tenuous and all too brief hold on mortality. But tumor? To hear the word directed at our own body, or the body of a loved one? A chill, a shiver, the casting of bones, an omen of doom. Our very dictionaries intimate the worst. A tumor "arises without obvious cause and possesses no physiologic function." "An abnormal mass of tissue that results from excessive cell division...uncontrolled and progressive." "A morbid enlargement."

A self-generated, uncontrolled, morbid enlargement has been swallowing Linda's speech.

"For it to be this big, it must have been growing a long time," remarks Dr. de Boer while his assistant phones the admitting hospital, books a room, and schedules surgery.

In meticulous detail, he explains that the tumor's size prevents air from vibrating the vocal cords, which is how speech is created. He worries that the weight of it has already damaged her cords beyond repair. He makes her understand that even a week's delay places her in further jeopardy.

Through all this, Linda is giddy with relief.

She is not one of Freud's patients, one of those passive Victorian women flattened by patriarchal power, constrained to express themselves through hysterical symptoms! She has a real identifiable condition — a cystic tumor, said Dr. de Boer — enormous, the size of a pumpkin, inside her throat. Benign, but enormous. It's not her fault that she squeaks instead of sings, nor that the queen in Sam's story is mute, nor that this, or any other, narrative lacks structure. It's not her fault that her voice lacks authority.

She calls Daniel. As she explains what's happening, she is conscious of the diminished trickle of air barely passing over her cords. The breathiness is amplified like wind in her ears. "The doctor says it's amazing any sound comes out." She is becoming inaudible, fatigued at the effort required by this much conversation.

Concerned, dismayed, preoccupied, Daniel forgets to ask any questions.

An operation thrusts you to center stage. Linda, reluctant though she is, must become the star of her own drama, at least until the crisis is over. It's a new role. Sam's worried little face greets the news. He is scared something bad will happen to her in the hospital. She reassures him that she'll be all right. This is not necessarily true. Anesthesia has its own danger, even if Dr. de Boer's hand is steady.

"How do they get the knife in?" asks Sam. "Will they cut your throat?"

She explains that the knife is very tiny, and it's on the end of a tube with a prism and a camera, and, manipulated from outside by the doctor, it will push back her epiglottis and find her vocal cord and remove the tumor. She has trouble imagining it, herself. A tiny knife? When Dr. de Boer explained about micro-laryngoscopy and the microsurgical instruments he'll be using, and the camera, she nodded yes, but her mind closed down, his words floating past her, as if the anesthesia had already been administered.

"He's putting a camera down your throat?" Sam is astonished.

"So that he can take a picture of the tumor. A before and after."

Sam decides this is really cool and plans to tell his class during share time the next day.

The news about Linda spreads. Friends and relatives phone or text. Some leave social media messages; the circle of the concerned grows wider and wider. Daniel's mother calls. "What can I do? What do you need?" Linda's cousin who lives in Newport emails, "Is it malignant? What if you can never speak again?" Daniel's sister-in-law barks into the phone, "Just tell me exactly what the doctor said. Verbatim." Linda develops pat phrases about how lucky she was to have caught it in time, etc., etc. One phone call takes her aback, from a well-known director, one of the many she'd met over the years, through Daniel of course. They'd socialized occasionally, at fancy restaurant dinners with his wife, a star on an edgy cable show. It never crossed her mind this man knew she existed apart from those meals.

"Don't do it!" he says, after the prerequisite hellos. "Your voice will be ruined. You'll become one of those shrill ball-busting women."

There is a pause in which she does not respond. Finally, she manages a dry, "Thank you for that," and hangs up.

If she hadn't been so busy organizing her hospital visit, she might have called him back and said in her whispery voice that he did not have a proprietary interest in how she sounded, that her speech was not designed for his pleasure, that her laryngal health was more important to her than his opinion and that he could go fuck himself. Or maybe not. To date, Linda has never been that direct.

She makes the arrangement for Sam to stay with Daniel's parents, so Daniel can be with her during surgery. She plans what she'll need for the hospital. The process is arduous. It reminds her of writing. She has to imagine herself in a place she's never been, and then provide the necessary objects. Modest pajamas and a terry robe. Slippers for cold floors. Her favorite sweatpants. No turtlenecks, nothing tight that has to be pulled over her head, in case her throat can't take the pressure.

She avoids thinking about what her throat will be like, how defenseless it will be.

Daniel is still making his way through the One Hundred Best Books list. But there is a message for her on his iPad: I downloaded some reading material I think you'll like. She is flooded with affection. Daniel has not stifled her voice; a tumor has. Daniel isn't worried that she will become a shrill ball-busting woman. She searches for the travel alarm clock he gave her on her thirtieth birthday with the note tucked in the leather case that said, "I'd travel through time to be with you.'"

"Socks," she reminds herself. "Don't forget socks. And yellow pads to write on."

Everything goes into a small red duffel bag.

Stephanie brings over a stack of magazines and a playlist of Latin favorites on her first-generation gold iPod Touch. Beginning when they met in Junior High where Stephanie, daughter of the Mattress King of the Northwest Valley, interspersed 'you know' and 'like' between every sentence fragment, even though she tested gifted and aced trig in the ninth grade, Linda has observed her friend's many incarnations, but never this commitment. Not only the dancing — the meringues and sambas and rumbas in clubs all over the county — but the change of hair color, the darkened eyebrows, and the wardrobe switch from expensive designer clothes to spicy Latin dance outfits. She and her salsa partner are now regulars on semi-pro circuits, entering and winning contests.

Stephanie drops the magazines on the bed. Linda, who is arranging flowers, hands her a silver rose with a sweet, citrusy scent that Daniel once called intoxicating. She hopes the arrangement and the scent will make him feel less lonely while she's in the hospital. Stephanie means to tell Linda that she saw Daniel the other night. She's been saving it, a conversational morsel — what a coincidence, off the beaten track, such a funky Tex-Mex bar. Unfortunately, in her anxiety over Linda's tumor, she forgets. She obsesses about tumors and pricks her finger on the rose.

"I'm going to get blood poisoning!"

"You'll be fine." Linda's reassurance is automatic. "Just suck on it."

Linda places the rose in the vase with four others, just starting to open. For once, she's satisfied with the effect.

"People can die from blood poisoning," Stephanie stresses.

Linda doesn't state the obvious — that of the two, she is the one who will be on the operating table. She hugs her friend, goes to the medicine cabinet, takes out an alcohol wipe she uses for Sam's scrapes, pats the dot of blood, then finds a Tweetie-Bird Band-Aid and wraps it around Stephanie's finger.

"I wish they had Tweetie-Bird Band-Aids for tumors," weeps Stephanie.

Before going to bed, Linda puts on the pale ivory lace negligee Daniel gave her for Valentine's Day a year ago.

She hardly ever wears it. There have been times when she's started to put it on, then folded it back in its tissue, embarrassed by how it could be read as an announcement of her desire for sex. But tonight, its filmy delicacy suits her mood. She wants to be cherished, treated like precious crystal that must be handled very carefully or it will shatter. She wants to be Elizabeth Barrett Browning, at least for one night. She doesn't tell this to Daniel, of course, because, in her reverie, if she did, he would say, "Shush, darling, don't strain your voice." And in a chapter worthy of a romance novel, he would take her into his arms and kiss the hollow of her throat, and suffuse each cell of her body with tenderness and desire, and arousal would build, a symphony reaching climax, replete with French horns and kettle drums, until she fell away from herself, ego dispersing into sensation.

Daniel doesn't notice the transparent nightgown, or the perfume she has dabbed between her breasts. He misses the invitation in Linda's face, the way her hair falls onto a half-bare shoulder. His libido is preoccupied. This does not mean he won't make love to her. He wants to, desperately, but the desperation comes across as neediness, and she recoils from his cold and clammy touch.

She doesn't know that he is flailing in a sea of angora.

A drowning man, he wants her to rescue him from his shame — not the shame of the act committed, but of his urge to do it again. Even while she, his wife, the mother of his child, is scheduled to go under the knife, he is calculating how many nights she'll be in the hospital, and how much time that gives him with Rosie.

Linda rolls over to her side of the bed.

Daniel pursues her across the Egyptian cotton sheets. Not just his hands, his entire body is cold and clammy.

She shivers. He assumes she's excited. His fingers reach between her legs. She tries to push him away. She wants her Daniel back, the one with the warm skin that heats her heart, the one who sends her into giggles during fore-play, and who then, deft and sure, converts the giggles into something more. That Daniel hasn't been around in a while, she realizes, as she tries to twist out from under him.

"What's wrong?" he asks.

She can't tell him. Not right before she goes into the hospital. "Will you miss me?" she queries, instead.

In the dark, she misses his expression, the way he side-steps her question with what passes for humor.

"Maybe I won't recognize you without the tumor."

## 16. Will

The Korean-born Nurse Cho smells like kimchi, which Linda would eat, having read about the benefits produced by the fermentation process, but she doesn't like how it tastes, too much heat.

"You read Schopenhauer? Very gloomy man, but smart. Deep. I say he's very deep, what do you say?"

A copy of The World as Will and Idea is in her hand, which she waves in Linda's face. Korean is not a soothing sounding language, and even in English, the nurse's voice is not soothing. Linda wants the hospital to be calm and quiet. She wants tranquil music, comforting hands. The pungent smell of garlic and chili gives Linda a headache. The nurse puts the book down and scrubs her hands.

"Schopenhauer?" Linda dredges back in her memory to first year philosophy, but a reply is unnecessary because the nurse sticks a thermometer in her mouth.

"We must assert the Will," says Nurse Cho. "How do you think I leave my country? My father tries to stop me. United States is not good for girls, too many rapists. But I assert the Will. Rapists everywhere, I say, even Korea."

She finishes taking Linda's temperature. An orderly comes in with the gurney.

"You have operation soon." Nurse Cho checks the chart. "Dr. de Boer — he is excellent surgeon. He'll do excellent job with your appendix."

Linda bolts up. "There's nothing wrong with my appendix!"

Nurse Cho laughs. "Hospital joke."

Under his dreadlocks, the orderly grins at the woman's short, wide, departing back. "She's the best nurse on the floor," he assures Linda, a fact she is relieved to hear.

"Schopenhauer," she murmurs and shakes her head.

Too complex for her to ponder when facing the perils of surgery, she flips through Stephanie's old magazines. Fashion. Diet. Finance. Exercise. Celebrities. Health. Graffiti of the mind.

The orderly leaves before she can ask if she ought to draw a circle on her throat, with a red arrow pointing to her vocal cord. She didn't pack any of Sam's magic markers, which means she'd have to request one. That requires too much energy. She places her head to the pillow. She closes her eyes. She might as well sleep, and dream of the new voice that will emerge once surgery is over. A strong voice, not a ball-busting one.

"Knock, knock!" Daniel comes in, bringing Linda a basket of Mrs. Beasley's lemon muffins and a giant bouquet, "From the head of CBS," he says. "Plus, there are more at home, waiting for you. From HBO, Netflix, and at least three agencies."

They aren't really for her. Hollywood is using her surgery as a way to curry favor with Daniel, so he'll continue posting favorable articles about the shows and talent on the air.

A push of a button automates her bed. "Daniel," she asks, as it moves to an eighty-degree angle, "Have you ever read Schopenhauer?"

"I always recommend him before an operation."

She smiles. He looks good. Fresh, outdoorsy, color in his cheeks. The opposite of a hospital. She stretches out her arms for a hug.

Daniel buries his nose in a bouquet sent by Linda's parents who moved to Asheville and don't seem to miss anyone in California, they're having such an active and interesting time.

"Nice flowers."

Her arms drift back down.

"Sam says hello." He sounds strained.

It must be the hospital, she figures. People become awkward in hospitals. They stiffen, even husbands. Especially husbands.

"You told him I'll be okay?"

"He was too busy explaining about the tiny knife going down your throat."

She smiles again.

Minutes later, the orderly reappears. It's time. Daniel pecks Linda on the cheek and hastily wishes her luck. He looks miserable. Since we have withheld the Daniel-Rosie sub-plot from Linda, and the angora lint has been forgotten in the drama of her tumor, she mistakes his hangdog expression for concern about her operation. Linda tries to reassure him by waving cheerfully as the orderly wheels her past the front desk, past Nurse Cho, past a Candy Striper pushing a chrome cart lined with trays of pink and green and yellow squares of Jell-O.

Without mishap, they reach the prep area. Needles are placed in her veins; propofol drips in. Dr. de Boer greets her. The Pre-Op Nurse tells her she's in good hands. Linda believes her.

The last time she had anesthesia, she was four. That doctor made her count to ten. At number seven she couldn't speak any more, but she was still conscious, and she was terrified they'd think she wasn't and start cutting her tonsils out. That childhood fear reasserts itself. She forces her eyes to stay open, signaling consciousness. In spite of her efforts they close. A cool soothing sensation sweeps over her.

"Wiggle your fingers," she hears through the mist.

One finger manages to move. Then, even that low level of activity ceases. No longer worrying about brain damage from aspiration or airway trauma or bronchospasm, casting aside any Schopenhauerean potential for actualizing the Will, her mind slides away, into a vacant, amiable darkness.

While Dr. de Boer photographs, snips, slices, and photographs again, Linda is absent. The success or failure of the surgery has nothing to do with her participation. She is the raw material for his accomplishment, more inert than a chunk of granite or a piece of wood where at least the striation of the surface or the pattern of the grain has some influence on the finished product.

The 'before' and 'after' photos will come out. Even though the camera is microscopic, the photographs will be the size of Polaroids. The Before: Linda's tumor — a large blue-white milky ball blocking air space — attached to the surface of the vocal cord. The After: Linda's vocal cord — without the tumor — clean and smooth, surrounded by space.

Dr. de Boer will give the photos to Linda, emphasizing what he had already anticipated, that the tumor — cystic, growing unchecked for the last fifteen years — was benign, although by no means innocuous. She will do the calculations quickly. The tumor began when she started college. It predated her marriage.

She'll label the photo with the tumor, WILL.

"Look at Will," she'll say. "Such determination." Sam'll be the only one who listens. "All balled up, ignored by everyone, growing in moist mucosal secrecy, until…" A long pause.

"What?" Sam will plead.

"Until, finally, it's Will's very silence that makes it heard."

The other photo will be labeled, WITHOUT WILL.

# 17. Hospitality

While Hospitalism is a condition that arises from spending too much time in a hospital, hospitality is a condition that arises from the mere act of being in a hospital. It is not a matter of choice. Like lemmings, visitors from the outside world navigate blindly through monolithic buildings and confusing corridors to the room where the patient is secured, if not by tubes and IVs, then by the body's infirmity. They bring candy or flowers and expect to be welcomed by someone who has been betrayed by one's physical self and is hardly in the mood.

When Linda awakens in the Recovery Room, she is told that her husband has gone out, but that her best friend, Stephanie, is waiting. Her mind is too fogged to wonder where Daniel has gone. She is too thirsty to care about anything except drinking water, which, apparently, she's not supposed to have. She might as well be in the desert, in Death Valley, for god's sake, where the road sign reads "no water or gas for the next 60 miles" (or is it the next 160 miles?), where people who don't have water to drink die of thirst.

"Mrs. Gregory," begins the Recovery Room Nurse — a West Bengali woman whose name-tag reads Chandrakanthra Mukherjee.

Linda doesn't respond. We haven't trained her to think of herself as a Mrs. Gregory. Nobody, not even her all lesbian Ace-1 cleaning crew, calls her that.

Nurse Mukherjee taps her shoulder. "You do understand how important it is not to use your voice, not for an entire month?"

At the end of the month, sound will be reintroduced to

her vocal cords. De Boer has explained this.

She doesn't die of thirst, after all, because Nurse Mukherjee brings her ice cubes and makes sure her brain has resumed its normal functioning. She is more sympathetic than the Recovery Room Nurse Linda had at age four who yelled at her for crying and told her if she didn't stop, her parents would leave her in the hospital. Linda called her a liar, even though she'd been instructed not to speak. The nurse threatened to withhold ice cream. Linda kept her mouth shut after that.

Back in her room, all she wants to do is doze. She barely is aware of Nurse Cho's gentle ministrations or of Stephanie, patiently doing needlepoint — an Elvis pillow for her mom who never accepted his death. After an hour, more or less — Linda has no sense of time, minutes bending into days, lifetimes — she musters the energy to write, "Hi," on one of the yellow pads. The H is slanted, the I is wiggly, and the pencil drifts off the page without the energy for a period or exclamation point. Suffering from a post-anesthesia headache, she does not desire conversation, but now that she has shown signs of life, Stephanie takes it upon herself to relate the particulars of the rose thorn episode.

"The doctor said to watch for red streaks going up my arm so I spent the entire day watching." Stephanie shows Linda her pale, smooth arm. "It's fine. I'm fine. Your hydrogen peroxide and Tweetie-Bird Band-Aid did the trick." She bursts into tears. "I'm so glad you made it through surgery!"

Daniel returns, saving Linda from more of Stephanie's emotional upheavals, although why he had to leave for so long makes no sense, since most of his business is conducted on the phone, and his cell phone practically grows out of his head.

Stephanie blows her nose before she addresses Daniel. "Fluky coincidence, wasn't it?"

"What?"

"Seeing you at that bar. I thought I was the only one who knew about that place!"

Even through her post-operative haze, and the hammering of her temples, Linda perceives a change in Daniel's countenance. His skin blotches; his jaw shifts back and forth. His voice is too loud when he says, "Hell, if I know what you're talking about."

"You know, that bar in Hollywood, with the Tejano music, and rot-gut tequila."

Daniel's shoulders shrug all the way to his ears in perplexed bewilderment. "Sounds great. Where is it?"

Stephanie glances at Linda and unscrews the cap on the pink glitter nail polish she's brought to give her best friend a pedicure — her specialty since 8th grade. "Near Fountain and Normandie. I could have sworn it was you, but that's what I get for having one shot too many. All Anglos start to look alike!"

Linda watches Daniel's face return to its normal color. He runs his fingers through his hair.

"Can I get you anything?" he asks her, solicitously.

"Yeah, a diet coke," answers Stephanie.

"I meant Linda. How are you feeling, sweetheart?"

Sweetheart washes over her like a tide on its way out, leaving a residue of wet scum. She closes her eyes.

"Maybe we should go and let her get some rest," Daniel suggests.

Stephanie dutifully screws the nail polish top back on.

Linda wants nothing more than to sink down into the white sheets of oblivion. However, Nurse Cho bustles back in, stopping the departure of her visitors.

"You hear this one?" she asks, once again placing a thermometer in Linda's mouth. "The patient say to doctor: 'Doc, there's a rectal thermometer behind your ear!' 'Damn,' say Doctor, 'some asshole must have my pencil.'"

Nonplused, Stephanie and Daniel stare at Nurse Cho.

"You the husband?" she asks Daniel. "You married smart lady."

He agrees, energetically.

"We talk Schopenhauer before surgery." She wags her index finger at Linda. "Only no talking now, you hear! Very important." Turning back to Daniel, "You know Schopenhauer?"

Daniel manages to keep a straight face. "Not personally."

"He makes a joke. I like him!"

Nurse Cho removes the thermometer and takes Linda's blood pressure.

"What I find brilliant about Schopenhauer," volunteers Stephanie, unexpectedly, but then, Linda recalls, her friend always had been drawn to 19th century German philosophy, even before the trend of deconstructing meanings, "is his notion that you create your own reality by willing it to be." Stephanie adjusts the strap of her shoulder bag. "Since reality is all so subjective, anyway."

She blows Linda a kiss, and leaves.

Linda weakly raises a hand to stop her. She wants to argue, if reality is so subjective, why do narratives go amiss when they flout logic?

Supposing, right now, at this juncture, a terrorist leapt in through the hospital room window and held them hostage until Nurse Cho released the secret formula for a genetically superior turnip? Would readers believe it? Not likely. It wouldn't be real.

And by the same token, no matter how much she tries to will it away, she knows that Daniel reacted when Stephanie mentioned the Tejano bar. She knows, from the expression on his face, that he's been there. No matter what Stephanie postulates, there is that reality — objective, un-transmutable, non-Schopenhaurean reality.

If this were a detective story, she would pursue why Daniel had gone to that particular bar, either flatfoot it herself, or hire a private eye to find out. But it's not a detective story. Unless she wills otherwise. And right now, post-surgery, that seems far-fetched.

Her eyes smart. She wants Daniel and Nurse Cho to go before she actually cries.

Get out, she wills them. Both of you.

Alas, she is, for the moment, without will.

Anyway, Daniel can't leave. An unexpected visitor is about to arrive, and he needs to meet her.

"Hello! May I come in?" chirps a woman in a bright yellow pantsuit, her hair down, clipped on either side by a Chinese enamel butterfly.

Linda almost doesn't recognize her therapist, who she's seen only in loose rayon dresses, mauve with hints of pale blue, with her hair up, and wearing horn rimmed glasses.

Dr. Raven stands at the threshold, looking at Linda, through her, focusing on her auras, no doubt, and a rogue cloud of suspicion concerning Daniel, hovering, going nowhere.

She introduces herself.

Daniel stares. "I thought this wasn't allowed, the two of us meeting. Against the rules."

Faith takes that as an invitation to walk in.

"You must be Daniel, Linda's husband."

## 18. Angora sex

The wool of angora rabbits should be trimmed before it grows too long, otherwise when the rabbits lick themselves clean, too much gets in their mouth, and they choke to death on oversized hairballs.

But wait. First things first. The promised digression.

When it happened, Rosie knew it wouldn't be in a hotel. She didn't want Daniel spending any money because then she would be obligated to him, instead of the other way around. Moreover, this was not going to be some sleazy furtive one-day stand. Daniel had to see her as a real person, with needs of her own, with a career to be helped. He had to experience where she lived — a modest but charming studio apartment in the flats, scented by sage and lavender, decorated with folk masks from around the world, a collection inherited from her grandmother, who Rosie adored. She does not intend to bring up Warner Records and Daniel's deception-by-omission because she knows he is a better man than that.

After he agrees to meet her, she lights the Laundromat candle. The flickering light gives Saint Mary Magdalene a lovely glow. Rosie slips on a pink angora sweater that matches the angora afghan, hand-knit from Wales, tossed at the foot of her bed. Rosie likes angora; it reminds her of the 50s, a time long before she was born but one with which she feels an affinity. She wears a very short skirt, sans underwear, and her sexiest shoes. She selects music — jazz instrumental. She'll provide the vocals.

Is Rosie nervous? Nope. Sex has always been a game for her. She's picked up men in bars, and in traffic — BMWs and Mercedes, no vans. She's copulated in airplanes and

Laundromats, during dinners at fancy restaurants and at the Philharmonic. She's done it as a threesome. She's played hooker on Sunset Boulevard when a friend dared her to do it with him for money — $150 plus tip. She's been hurt, of course, by falling for the rake's smile and a fast ride in a Porsche across the Mojave, but not often, and she's never been abused or pregnant. She's no saint, but there's no need of excuses. She embraces appetite.

She goes to Daniel's website, his name in large font, a definite thrill. She scrolls through an article about a silver-screen seductress with rosebud lips who "has carved a niche for herself in the fashion pages of our nation's tabloids — where her assets are frequently on display in increasingly bizarre outfits." Rosie's not jealous of the starlet who, without talent, has only her body to sell. Daniel has more refined taste. She looks for evidence of his input. He must have commissioned the latest interview with an actress who never married the father of her children: "I'm not trapped in my relationship. We're individuals who, every day of our lives, wake up and choose to be together." Rosie appreciates the sentiment. She and Daniel are choosing to be together, this very afternoon. The actress goes on to say: "I want to know where joy lives. You know, a baby smiles something like seventy-two times a day. Where does that smile go?"

Rosie doesn't really care about those seventy-two smiles. She just needs to put one on Daniel's face.

He arrives.

A Vodka martini. An obligatory inspection of carved wooden masks, some with feathers, others with mother of pearl teeth. Segue to the couch. The prickling of goosebumps on his skin when she sings along with Duke Ellington. Her voice, gliding up and down his entire body, insinuating itself into erogenous zones he didn't know he possessed.

His inability to restrain himself, picking her up, mid-phrase, burying his nose in the pink fluff of her angora sweater, practically racing to the bed, never letting go of her, not now, not when his arms finally are holding the body that houses the voice that so captivates him, and certainly not after he makes the discovery, once they fall on the bed, that under her short fetching skirt she has nothing on, absolutely nothing but the welcome of her sweet moist sex, unfolding with anticipation. His loafers sliding off, and slacks, and beneath the pink angora, finding her breasts, the two most deliriously perfect objects he's ever kissed, and she, tilting, so the nipples reach his mouth, suckling at the temple of goddess Aphrodite, an act of holy ecstasy, and then, her hands on his cock — all he can do is moan and moan again until with a quick little movement she turns upside-down, her lips touch the head, a full throaty sound, she takes it in her mouth and she circles her tongue around its circumference – and her hands are cupping his testicles and his fingers clutch blindly the angora afghan tangled in their passion and he reaches for her and thrusts her over above his cock never this stiff never this hot never in his entire life and plunges her down on him impaling, piercing, penetrating and his hands enclose her waist and he lifts her higher and lower and he arches and bucks and she rides him and her palm presses above his pubic bone and with a poignant cry he curses because the pleasure is so intense and it has to end because he can't control it anymore.

They lie there, the angora sticky with his semen and her cum because, once he caught his breath, he plied his palm to her mound, his fingers in her cunt, and teased and pressed and rubbed until her body spasmed and her own hot fluid gushed out between her legs.

Unable, unwilling to move, they lie there, enveloped by sticky angora.

Linda unwraps the gift from Faith. She puts it on the lam-
inate bed table, a touch of nineteenth century decor amidst
the monotone beige and disposable plastic of twenty-first
century hospital rooms. Hand-painted red robins warbling
black musical notes on a forest green tin containing imported English butterscotch. While she speculates on what
it'll be like to suck the hard candy — sweet juice trickling
down her esophagus, circumventing recently ravaged tissue, because, as she keeps reminding herself, vocal cords
aren't located inside the esophagus — Dr. Raven folds her
hands together and comes to the point.

"Linda, I know I won't be seeing you until you're speaking again, but, in the interim, I'd like permission to write
about your case."

Linda doesn't even try to open the tin of candy; she's
too weak.

The therapist explains to Daniel how she had sensed
there was something wrong with Linda's voice.

"Interesting how things show up in analysis."

She gives analysis the credit, though she's confident
most analysts wouldn't have seen it, certainly not the aura
of pain that was so vivid to her.

"Naturally, the identity would remain anonymous, but I
believe the work we did is very important…"

Linda's mind vacates. She hears what Faith is saying,
and she is aware that Daniel is glowering, but Faith's words
have nothing to do with Daniel's glower. There is a discon-
nect. If it's not in her mind, then it's in the room. She wishes
Daniel would stop glowering. It makes his brows too close
and shortens his forehead and purses his lips. She wants

Faith to see how attractive he is; she wants her to have a true picture, not a scowling one.

"You intend to exploit my wife's medical history?"

Righteous outrage over violation of privacy. A display Linda finds paradoxical, given the nature of Daniel's work— he is the one responsible, after all, for churning out lurid profiles that feed paparazzi frenzy.

"And profit from it?" Daniel rolls his eyes upward, as if only the pale cream acoustic tile of the hospital ceiling could adequately appreciate how appalled he is.

"Well, there's no money involved, but, as a matter of fact, yes, I would like other people to profit from our experience."

Faith takes Linda's hand into her own soft palms. "You don't have to make a decision until you've recuperated, dear. I just wanted you to think about it."

Dr. Raven is being disingenuous. For days, she's been absorbed by the prospect of writing the article; its focus will be on the role of intuition as a diagnostic tool. She is convinced that if her inner eye hadn't perceived the injury Linda's vocal cords would have become damaged beyond repair. She has transcribed all the notes from their therapy sessions, augmenting some from memory. She has photographed the nodules of clay tagged with the names Linda had given them and printed out the fairy tale she'd told her child. If Dr. Raven is successful and keeps to her schedule, she might publish her version of Linda's story before Linda has the opportunity to finish this one.

Her hand swoops towards Linda's throat.

A talon, thinks Daniel, a talon for the doctor appropriately named Raven. He scowls — not much different from a glower — as if his own space is being violated.

Linda's throat. There are no more swirls of color, no angry reds or pulsating orange. The air is lit solely by rays of light slanting in through standard issue hospital blinds. Faith gently lays a palm on the side of the neck and directs her energy flow toward the wound.

Daniel's scowl deepens.

"Can we talk somewhere else, so Linda can get some sleep?"

Linda shrivels at the prospect of the two of them conversing.

Faith pats her shoulder. "Heal quickly. I'll stay in touch."

They leave Linda to struggle with the sheet stretched too tightly across her feet, while her brain conjures the encounter she fears they will have in the hospital cafeteria.

Their encounter, as imagined by Linda:

The cafeteria is bathed in fluorescent light. Skin is sallow. Lipstick is garish. Glazed eyes combat the flickering of fluorescent tubes. Happy people do not eat in hospital cafeterias. Except, Linda modifies, those who have just had babies.

Faith dislikes fluorescent light, and avoids it whenever possible, but she's willing to put up with it in order to have a conversation with Daniel.

"This is not a level playing field," he launches in. "After all the stuff about me that Linda must've said, you've got the advantage."

A forced laugh, as if he's told a bad joke.

"Since we're here," says Faith, "I might as well have tea. What would you like?"

Daniel allows her to buy him a coffee.

They sit across from each other, the puke-green walls stretching — so far as Daniel is concerned — like an endless bad dream from which he will never escape.

"I wasn't aware this was a contest," Faith finally responds.

For a minute Daniel doesn't reply. His eyes narrow. He studies the older woman. He tries to decide if the bright yellow pantsuit turns her into a banana. Yes, he decides, it does, oozing potassium. A personal opinion, to be sure. Also, those butterflies holding up her long gray hair. Incongruous. Was she thinking to cheer Linda up? And yet, he acknowledges, even as a fruit bowl with insects in her hair, she'd do a better job than he's been doing.

He lowers his gaze into the god-awful cup of coffee. "Maybe you can explain why my wife is so unhappy, because she sure doesn't tell me."

"Is she so unhappy?"

Before Linda started therapy, Daniel hadn't thought so. He'd thought everything was fine.

"Maybe angry is a better word. Though, again, I don't see why. Unless she's angry she married me."

Another defensive laugh. He can't help it. That's his nightmare. That Linda is blaming him for her life because in one moment of youthful passion she had agreed "to love and cherish until death do them part".

"How did you meet?"

He thinks a minute, rumpling his hair with nervous fingers.

"She was licking a strawberry ice cream cone. The sun illuminated her face. It was one of those days. She was so vibrant."

That is not how Daniel met Linda.

Readjusting her pillow, unable to find a comfortable position on the awkward inhospitable hospital bed, Linda adjusts the answer.

"No, wait, it was in a seminar," Daniel tells Faith. "Linda was attacking Arthur Miller for the patronizing way he wrote the Marilyn Monroe character in After the Fall, but her voice... you know, that breathiness... she sounded just like Marilyn, only with a brain... a potent combination. I fell for it, along with everyone else. Why? What'd she say?"

"Who was the girl with the ice cream cone?"

"Linda. But it was some other guy who saw her." He shrugs. "Until he noticed her, I hadn't been interested. Funny how his description made her come alive." A pause. "We were all pretty young." Another pause. "And good-looking." A self-deprecating laugh, to which Faith doesn't respond. "I wonder if she regrets not marrying him."

"Do you regret marrying her?"

"Listen, Dr. Raven, until she started seeing you, I would have told you we were perfectly happy. Everything was going great. We had a great life. A great kid. Why would she want to mess with it? Look what happens!"

"What happens?"

Rosie. Rosie happens.

(Linda has fallen asleep. She is no longer in charge of this discussion. It continues without her.)

"Everything gets questioned," declares Daniel. "And before you realize it, what seemed like a solid structure becomes a house of cards. I'm beginning to have a lot of respect for the Victorians. They knew to let well enough alone. I don't see how any relationship holds up under scrutiny."

It's not Faith's place to argue with him about the efficacy of psychotherapy. She sips her tea.

Daniel feels cheated. He wants a confrontation. He wants to prove he's justified in seeing Rosie.

"How many of your patients' marriages break up after they start seeing you?"

Faith has never counted.

"Shouldn't you know? Isn't that an important statistic?"

"Are you afraid your marriage is going to break up?"

"Hey, this is not my therapy session!"

Faith smiles. "Sorry. It's a habit."

The smile softens him. He has a perverse desire to tell her about Rosie. She's a shrink; doesn't that mean she'd have to keep his confidence?

Rosie. If he leaves now, he'd make it to Joe's Diner in time for her break. Her top button would be undone. And then the next. They could go to the parking lot. Edged by hedges, enough privacy for intimate contact.... No. No. That won't do.

A husband sneaking out of the hospital on the heels of his wife's operation to have illicit sex with her singing teacher is a sleaze-bag, a cad. We'd be annoyed if Linda didn't find out and react, do something — call him a schmuck, kick him out of the house. If she remained oblivious, we'd turn against her, reject her as a blind fool who's getting what she deserves because, we'd flatter ourselves, in her situation, we would know, and we would do something.

When is it the right moment to give up on a marriage?

Linda and Daniel once loved each other; they have a son who means the world to both of them. She won't be able to speak for a month. Of necessity, that changes the dynamic between them. One way or another, shifts will take place.

Daniel keeps his mouth shut about Rosie. He fiddles with the napkin.

Faith sips her tea. "Therapy may be a catalyst, but it's never the actual cause of a break-up. If stale dynamics are challenged, it might be a good thing."

She pays no attention to her words. She is imagining her article: VOICE ISSUES, a case history, submitted by Faith

Raven, Ph.D., MFCC: Patient X, a warm attractive woman, married, with one child, seeking therapy because —

"Linda thinks our marriage is a stale dynamic?" Daniel's voice hollows out.

Faith puts down her cup. "That's not what I said."

"It's what you implied."

"Is it?"

"I'd better be getting back to my wife."

Instead of Rosie.

He wishes the trek back to the hospital room weren't such an ordeal.

# 20. The yellow pad

Silence gives her power. Everyone wants to read what's written on the yellow pad.

Right now, nothing.

The top sheets torn off; clusters of sentences crumpled into irregular balls that she tosses towards wastebaskets. Clichés. Throw-away words, hastily scrawled.

I'm okay.

No, it doesn't hurt.

Say something; just because I can't speak doesn't mean you can't!

She's unconcerned if a ball of paper misses the basket. It will be cleaned up by the all-lesbian Ace-1 cleaning crew. Daniel has asked them to come every day while she recuperates. Perhaps they un-crumple the pieces, reading words randomly. No. Okay. Speak. Mean it. Sequences that are no longer hers, creating a person completely unlike herself. Would it matter?

Marcel Proust paid attention to what he wrote. A real writer pays attention.

Linda suffers a wave of nausea. She must not be a real writer. There are no madeleines in this story.

The only one too impatient to wait for her to answer on the yellow pad is Daniel. He asks yes or no questions.

Since she's been home, he's been distracted.

Even Sam has noticed. "Daddy thinks he's reading to me, but he's not. He's just saying the words in the book."

She tells herself it's his work, which always has justified Daniel's preoccupied moments, although never before has it been so indiscriminate, such a sweeping excuse for major mood swings, anxiety attacks, expensive shirts in colors he's previously avoided — turquoise, neon yellow, even a hot pink— not to mention the purchase of a digital elliptical heart-saver machine.

"To relieve stress. I have a stressful job." Emphasis on 'stressful,' ready to take it to the mat if she expresses doubt.

He exercises his way through the eleven o'clock news and through late, late shows he never used to watch. Not until she's fast asleep does he climb in bed, carefully keeping to his side of the mattress.

He won't kiss her. He says he's worried he'll hurt her, but on Sunday morning when Sam is hunkered in his room, oblivious to everything but the Lego bat cave he's constructing, she scribbles Daniel a note. She misses him, his mouth, his body, and, she writes, his tongue isn't long enough to do any damage, could never, not even if it were as long as a lizard's.

He backtracks.

"I tried to spare you the truth. I'm not proud of it, but I can't help it. The real reason I don't kiss you," his eyes shift away from hers, "is I can't. When I think about the incision inside your throat, I freeze up."

He coughs loudly, and then mumbles something along the lines of how it makes him sick, how he can't handle the idea of a wound, especially one he can't see, especially in a woman, especially if the woman wounded is his wife.

Linda stares at her husband. What an awful thing to say.

"I make you sick?" she writes, pressing too hard on the pencil, breaking the point.

His face contorts. "Crazy, I know. Probably some Freudian fear of female genitalia as a wound thing. I'm sure your therapist can figure it out. I'll make it up to you. I promise."

She is too dumbfounded to respond.

Unable to stand another moment of the shocked expression on her face, he takes the silence as agreement, grabs a tennis visor and racquet and rushes off.

We could add a literary flourish here: cold air follows in his wake; out on the quiet street a murder of black crows. But Linda wouldn't notice. Shuffling, one foot in front of the other, her body angled slightly forward, her face tilted down, brooding, she heads for the bedroom.

She'd been wrong. His tongue could hurt her. It just had.

If only she'd countered back. Something along the line of, "Female genitalia as a wound thing? What a crock!" She's read about vagina dentata— a male phobia common in folk tales and horror stories, as well as in psychoanalysis, the fear of the vagina having teeth, a fear of female power, sexual or otherwise, and the ensuing danger of castration. The 'wound thing?' According to Freud, that meant she'd already been castrated, her hypothetical original penis sliced off, and the boy/male seeing the results instinctively clutches his own organ and runs off, terrified it will happen to him.

She reaches the bedroom, oblivious to its stale smell, dispirited that she had not printed in large, hostile letters, "Get yourself a shrink". Did he wish she'd kept the tumor and let her voice disappear altogether?

It's too bad Linda doesn't follow up, scribble notes, record her reactions. A month's worth of notations will be chucked, a careless dismissal of scrawls, doodles, to-do lists, games with Sam — tic-tac-toe and hangman — as well cryptic clues to her interior moods. If she kept them, they could be collaged into the middle of this novel, framed by topics, or questions, or meditations. A palate cleanser. Or cookie crumbs showing the way. The trail.

"What constitutes voice?"

The question made poignant by her own voicelessness. Lists of possible answers.

1. Shouts. Whispers. Utterances. Whines. Speech. Orations. Singing, of course.

2. Style. Choices. Action. Reflection.

3. Opinions. Votes. Influence. Money.

It's not too late. She could staple all the sheets of paper together under the title 'Silence.' However cryptic or enigmatic, within a section labeled 'Silence' anything goes. By virtue of placement, incoherent fragments become coherent. Take the following observations: Robert Irwin, an artist, spent weeks alone on Ibiza, not talking to a living soul, and those were the weeks in which he learned to truly see. Or, for instance, the sound of AUM, which supposedly contains all the sounds of the universe, the final sound, coming after the vibration of M, is the fourth sound – the one of silence, the most powerful sound of all, although Linda never was one to chant AUM, not even when Stephanie was obsessed with affirmation mantras, and convinced AUM was the answer to all of life's questions.

Now place these observations next to "fold the laundry", one of Linda's household chores. We will look for threads of connection. That's what we humans do.

Linda reaches the bedroom. Its dim light and drawn blinds are a relief. Since she's been home from the hospital, the house has seemed too big, too bright, too flooded with options. She finds herself retreating, not because she's an invalid — in spite of Daniel's reaction, none of her internal organs have been maimed — but because the room is contained; it's manageable. The rest of the house is too open, a sprawling flow from kitchen to dining room to living room. Here in the bedroom the sound of the outside world is muffled. The rectangular boundaries of the mattress console her. There are reassuring nature shows on PBS — like the one about the songs of the humpback whales — that help her feel less disconcerted.

She's glad Sam is preoccupied with his bat cave. Usually, he bounces in after her. She has to lean against the pillows in order to keep her balance. Her son reminds her of particles colliding against each other in random confusion. She can't tell him that his energy is too much for her; that he follows her around like a rambunctious puppy when all she wants is peace and quiet. She can't do that. He's too concerned. At dinner last night, while they were all picking lethargically at Chinese take-out, he asked Daniel, "Will Mom ever be able to read to me again?" Daniel promised she would, but neither looked convinced.

Sam has heard his father's car leaving the house. Before Linda can relax, he runs into the bedroom. Is she okay? He doesn't say it aloud. He doesn't need to. His worried little face prompts a spasm of guilt. Carefully, in capital letters so it's easier for him to sound them out, she prints on her yellow pad: "CURL UP?"

She's not sure he can read the word curl. But curl he does, in a little ball, nestled under her armpit until, like a fire cracker, he explodes into action.

"I want to write!"

He grabs her yellow pad and takes the pen and prints SAM with the S facing the right way.

"Remember when I was little, I drew the S backwards? Remember how I had it go like a snake, sideways on the ground? Remember how I made the M like a W?"

He's stockpiling and organizing memories the way kids do with their collections of Pokemon or baseball cards.

Linda remembers the moment she knew she could read.

In kindergarten there was a poster with a picture of a cow, the word cow printed underneath. The cow, a brown and white Guernsey, floated in the air. No surrounding pasture. No milking machine. No calf. No cowboy. The picture's sole purpose was to illustrate the word. One day, during school nap time, she saw the letters c-o-w inside her head, all by themselves, without the picture, and she could tell that they spelled cow, that the word and the picture meant the same thing. Lying on a cot in a row with all the other kindergarteners, she tracked her brain as it rushed down synapses previously untraveled. Decades later, she can still recall that surge of recognition. Letters ceased being arbitrary. STOP. GAS. MILK. Wherever she went, there were letters, and the letters made words and words described the world; they described her in the world. She loved that about them. With her whole heart, with utter abandon, she loved letters. Their shape, how they could be combined, they were the calligraphy of the universe.

"Look what I wrote, Mom." Sam shows her the yellow pad.

He has printed "Sam, I am", in neat block letters.

She smiles. Sam's okay. He has a secure sense of himself. She cannot conceive of writing, "Linda, I am".

Then her child spurts the rest out loud, his big joke. "Green eggs and ham!"

Dr. Seuss. She wants to laugh, but she's not supposed to produce a single sound until Dr. de Boer says so. She'll share the moment with Daniel. He'll laugh for her. Unless her wound has stifled his laughter as well as his kisses.

Sam touches her throat, gingerly. "What does it feel like, Mom?"

She is stymied. Since she never felt the weight of the tumor, how can she feel the lack of it? If Sam had asked whether it hurt, reassuring him would be easy. But that's not what he wants to know. He has imagined the microscopic camera down his mother's throat, taking the before and after pictures. He's seen the tumor photos, Will and Without Will. He wants to know: What does the difference feel like?

Linda ruminates about empty space. Between the branches of trees, for instance. When the branches are cut down, what happens to that space?

If she loses her soul — something she's not sure she or anyone has — would she discover its presence by its absence?

Sam gets restless, waiting. He wants to jump up and down on the bed, but that's a no-no. He puts a pillow over his head. "Pretend I'm hiding, and you can't find me."

In cursive on her yellow pad, forgetting he can't read it, she answers his question. "I won't know until I can speak what it is that I feel."

By then, he has pushed the pillow away and returned to building his bat cave.

## 21. Death Valley

There is a choice.

We can let Linda recuperate from surgery at home, channel flipping like an exhausted barkless seal, trolling the internet to buy what she does not need, visiting and re-visiting Facebook, Instagram, Snapshot, or any other site that shows the happy people and their exciting lives —a contrast to her own dismal state. She'll write notes, either on the yellow pad or on the sleek new tablet that Daniel gives her to compensate for his inability to kiss her. Much tidier, says he, than paper spilling out of wastebaskets, consuming old growth forests, lighter as well, and more convenient than her computer. He has no comprehension of how much she appreciates the tactility of a pen or pencil in her hand pressing words onto a page. Or crossing them out because she's changed her mind or crushing the paper instead of hitting 'delete.'

While we wait patiently for her voice to return, we can wish that she'd throw nothing away, and that the pages or digital communiqués amount to more than a dry documentation of household minutiae, which, even if that holds a certain charm — i.e. get toilet paper, buy wild-caught Alaskan salmon for dinner, remind gardener to plant milkweed so monarchs will come — accumulated graffiti of a middle-class existence — it won't be the novel we are expecting, nor, frankly, the one we want.

We have another choice. Instead of focusing on minutia, we can enlarge the vista, expand horizons. We can take her out of the bedroom and drop her into a landscape that transforms a walk through a canyon into a mythic voyage. We can offer an environment that consumes extraneous matter, where the ordinary is stripped away until the only evidence of a life lived is its bleached bones. We can push her into a silence beyond her own, a silence so vast it swallows civilization.

We can send her to Death Valley.

Dr. Raven never has had a client who took a Jungian metaphor — the hero's journey, let's say — and made it literal. Linda would be a first. Would she advise against it, saying, "Look, dear, it's all very well in the safety of the therapist's office, but real life? You aren't one of the Prophets of old, wandering the desert for forty days."

Not likely. The opportunity for the Process of Individuation to unfold on multiple planes would be irresistible for a therapist like Dr. Raven. If Linda successfully completes The Hero's Journey, there will be a conclusion, not just for this book, but for Faith's own Voice Issues: A Case Study.

A question that may or may not occur to Dr. Raven or to Linda: When heroes go off alone to be challenged by the stuff of character, courage, or soul, are they being tested in extremis in order to uncover authentic abiding truths, or is it an escape from the myriad of minor difficulties that besiege their particular lives?

Stewing in her bedroom, Linda does not seek out Faith's advice. Nor does she participate in deliberations about possible narratives. She thumps her mattress; she mashes the comforter.

Slit. Gash. Crack. Cut.

The more she dwells on Daniel's recent aversion, his rhetoric of the vagina as wound, the more outraged and, yes, in spite of herself — humiliated — she becomes.

A few days pass. She can't let it go. Humiliation is not good for the healing process.

She e-mails her friend, Stephanie: "Can you believe

what an asshole?!"

Stephanie e-mails back: "Come salsa dancing."

Salsa dancing will not do the trick. However, Linda is done with her pity party. In a bold gesture of self-determination, consulting no one, she chooses her own course of action.

She e-mails Daniel at work that she has decided to go on a short trip so she can put a little distance between her wound and his neurosis. She e-mails the babysitter to pick Sam up from school and rearranges his schedule; she leaves her son a note with a happy face on the fridge, emphasizing how much she loves him and that she will be back Sunday night, and not to forget he has soccer, and Daddy will take him, and, if he misses her, he has permission to suck on the butterscotch candy in the green tin with the hand-painted birds, one piece, no more, for each day she's gone.

She throws a sleeping bag into the trunk of the car, along with a pair of red stiletto heels (for what? we wonder), two, no make that three, cases of bottled spring water with electrolytes, a stack of yellow pads, hiking boots, a large tube of sunscreen, and a wide-brimmed hat. She programs the GPS, and as back-up, finds an old AAA map of California in the garage, has the engine and tires checked, buys a sack of oranges at the freeway on-ramp, and heads for Death Valley National Park.

Past San Bernardino, out of urban traffic, her mind freed by cruise control, Linda's thoughts weave in and out of lanes at speeds almost too quick to follow. She tries to focus on Death Valley, a place she knows from childhood. She resists the sweet memory of her parents' van and the orange and blue tent where she and her sister cuddled in down sleeping bags. This is a hero's journey. The nostalgia of camp fires and roasting marshmallows, of lying on her stomach to lick the salt crystals in Bad Water Basin has to be replaced with new and powerful images: the descent into a Valley of Death, the resurrection on top of Funeral Mountain, and the return — telling Daniel to go fuck himself, her vagina is just fine, thank you very much.

But mental static crisscrosses random channels in her brain. The long drive and the straight road allow time for a quasi-dream state to take over, the zone when unconscious undercurrents swell into supercharged riptides of 'what ifs.'

What if the doctor's wrong, and the tumor was malignant and has already spread; what if Daniel has jinxed her recovery and she'll never speak again; what if men really do believe that vaginas are wounds.

Oblivious to the huge semi's torpedoing by, the frequency inside Linda's brain accelerates, sharp and clear, down treacherous routes.

What if she's alone, hiking through Marble Canyon, and she rounds a corner, and a man grabs her and pushes her against the polished limestone, and she struggles to get away, but he's too strong.

Attempts to deflect this particular 'what if' fail. The scenario hurtles along on its own momentum.

What if...

The man's knee pins her thigh. One hand clamps on her chest; the other yanks off her hiking shorts and underpants.

What if...

He whips out his penis like a switchblade, slicing at her crotch. She can't scream. She can't make a sound. Without a voice, she's helpless.

The tape repeats itself, rearranging the geography. In

the campground at night. On Devil's Golf Course. At Bad Water, two hundred and eighty-two feet below sea level. There are modifications. He pins her arms over her head. He holds her by the throat. He knocks her down onto lava rock, onto the sand dunes, the salt flats. And always, the presence of other Park visitors, oblivious to her scenarios.

The man has no distinguishing features. His clothes are Gap or Lucky Brand or LL Bean, ubiquitous, coated with dust and stained by sweat. She would not be able to recognize him in a lineup. In some versions — by this time Linda is long out of Barstow, zooming past billboards with pictures of Las Vegas casinos — Daniel is summoned away from that unacknowledged tejana bar with rot-gut tequila to pick her up at the police station or the hospital or the morgue where he sees her bruised and battered body.

Linda holds her breath and counts to ten. She knows this isn't going to happen. She releases her breath slowly. She has no intention of turning back; in fact, her resolve to spend a weekend in Death Valley is more fixed than ever, if only to prove to Daniel she can. But the tears keep flowing down her face and try as she might to visualize something reassuring — being a little girl again, playing dress-up with her sister, eating macaroni and cheese — she is unable to dislodge the vivid images of violation.

If Faith were in the car, she would tell Linda that a mythic journey, by its very nature, is fraught with risk, that her unconscious is preparing her for the psychic danger ahead. Transformation, Faith would add with a shake of her graying hair, is never safe.

A deceptive word, transformation. When dealing with our lives and the changes towards which we aspire, we assume that it is benign. We link it to Joseph Campbell and Robert Bly and psychoanalytical reinterpretations of fairy tales. Because we contemplate butterflies, rather than the mutilated cocoons of caterpillars, we don't perceive the violence within the word.

Linda can smell the oranges on the seat next to her. Oranges are optimistic, she decides, an early morning fruit promising a day full of health and vitality, a fruit that certainly can vanquish an imaginary rapist. She tears open the plastic sack. They spill out. She takes one and peels the thick skin, breaking the orange into sections. She is comforted by the sweet tart citrus flavor, an acid tang on the roof of her mouth, and by the white pith, the zest, and the sticky residue on her fingers and her lips.

Soon she will hit the stretch of highway posted with warnings — not about the dangers of transformation, but about gas and water. Be prepared, the signs imply, for this is a long and lonesome road without service stations or phones or tow trucks to rescue you if your car has stalled and your cell phone gets no reception. She pulls into Death Valley Junction, no more than a dot on a map, for a final fueling.

Just the hint of wind stirs the sagebrush and tamarisk trees. The town is empty. Not a soul wanders along the colonnade. The only signs of life are the gasoline pump and the Amargosa Opera House, the Junction's most famous landmark.

Linda knows nothing about Marta Becket, a classically-trained dancer, who, with her husband, discovered the abandoned opera house in Death Valley Junction while having a flat tire changed. "There was a magic to it," Marta is quoted as saying in a newspaper interview "and I thought to myself: 'This theater has got to be mine!'"

Linda, though she never read the article, is curious about the opera house which dominates the square. Leaving the car, she crosses over. A faded sign offers a brief history. Not satisfied with a peek through dirty windows, Linda pushes the door. It opens. She enters. The air is cool inside, and musty. Heavy drapes frame the small stage. She stares at figures painted on the walls — a stylized audience frozen in admiration for an aging Marta who had total faith in herself until she died at 92, who was committed to her art — however passé — performing nightly, whether people bought tickets or not. Her vital spirit, her life energy, is said to haunt the theater she'd made her own. Linda almost believes it.

She returns to the car and fills the tank. Perhaps the ghost of Marta Beckett watches from behind dusty crocheted curtains. A wraith wondering why this woman, alone, pumps gas in a town as deserted as Death Valley Junction. Does the sight of Linda inspire her to create a short ballet for an invisible audience, a piece in which a solitary woman approaches a gas pump? Who is to say? At first tentative, uncertain, afflicted with fear, the steps hesitant. An approach-avoidance pas de deux with the pump. By the end, intertwined with the hose, in charge of the nozzle, invigorated by the unleaded fuel, full of motion, does the spirit leap and whirl around the pump, until finally, unable to contain herself, race into the painted scrim of the desert?

Because Linda doesn't witness it, could not have witnessed it, nobody could have, unless in an altered state or another dimension, she has no idea whether or not her story, Linda's story, has been appropriated, given a narrative arc, and a final outcome. She proceeds as if the future is unknown, heading towards the horizon, submitting to its expanse, willing to fall off the edge.

She arrives at Furnace Creek campground before the

sun begins to set.

She stakes out her site by placing one of her yellow pads on a weathered picnic table and anchoring it with the pair of red stiletto heels.

Daniel can't concentrate. He's supposed to be planning a special issue of E-tainment for the Academy Awards, and his head is spinning. He never expected that Linda would take off like that, all because of his lame excuse about not kissing her. He could have made up something else — he was coming down with the flu and didn't want to infect her. Where did the female genitalia thing come from anyway? He loves vaginas. He loves the feeling of his penis inside them. He particularly and obsessively loves the feeling of his penis inside Rosie's vagina.

He can't see Rosie while Linda's gone. He has too much to do; he has to take care of Sam. Anyway, Rosie won't see him. He hasn't delivered on his promise. But he never promised. She just assumed he did. Maybe he should take her to the Oscars. Introduce her to stars. He could do that. Linda wouldn't care. She doesn't enjoy the glitz and glamour; she finds the evening boring, preferring to dish the celebrities at home with her friend, Stephanie. But if he leaves her alone with Stephanie, Stephanie might remember that she really did see Daniel with Rosie in that East Hollywood bar, and Linda would find out, and confront him, and his life would be in shambles.

Daniel wants to get off his mental roller coaster, but he can't. He's making himself sick. He's getting ulcers. Or acid reflux. His stomach's a mess. He should be on probiotics. How could Linda leave like that, right after surgery, without a voice? How crazy is she? If something happens, she won't be able to call him. She doesn't text. She hates texting. Would she text to save her life? He groans. Shit. He looks at the photo of him with Linda and Sam, taken in happier days, that sits on his desk. If something happens, it'll be his fault.

Chromium oxide green, zinc buff yellow, red iron oxide, chalky white. Hues from deep inside the earth. Linda stands on one of Death Valley's most popular bluffs, inhaling color.

Across the arroyo, a child, Sam's age — Linda's age when she started coming here as a girl — gallops along ribbon trails of aquamarine and russet and lavender, laced with saffron silica. The boy stirs up the dusty colors of the aptly named Artist's Palette and watches them settle on his hiking boots. Linda considers whether colors could become sounds. She may or may not be aware, depending on how much art history she has studied, that a century earlier, Wassily Kandinsky asked: "Which color is most similar to the singing of a canary, the mooing of a cow, the whistle of the wind...?" In any case, she hugs the issue close and makes it her own.

If she spoke with scarves of blue, and layered deep violet cardigans over crimson blouses, would Daniel take the time to listen?

The child waves. For a moment, it seems he's waving to her, beckoning, and she's tempted, but there's a parent on the bluff waving back, taking pictures. For now, it's enough to breathe. And breathe she does, great gulps of air, her diaphragm performing effortlessly, as if, all along, it's known what to do.

Oxygen incites appetite. She's hungrier than she's been in months. She leaves Artist's Palette, twilight muting rainbow hills into a pastel mauve, and she drives to the saloon at Furnace Creek Ranch for beef jerky or a pickled egg — something, anything they might have to eat.

At one table, downing pitchers of Sam Adams on draft, a group of boisterous college students compare off-road nightmares: "It was brutal — fifteen miles of high-speed meteorites!" "Dude ran out of gas in the gauntlet!" "Friggin' road kept its bad attitude."

Linda once suggested going off-road with Daniel and Sam, exploring otherwise inaccessible corners of the desert. But Daniel didn't want to.

"I'm a beach person," he claimed, as if one must choose. "Preferably a secluded beach in Tahiti, with you in a sarong."

The saloon door swings open. A man in a faded purple T-shirt walks in — that loping cowboy kind of walk made for Levi's and Stetsons, perfected by Clint Eastwood in those Italian westerns she'd watched with Daniel before they were married. This man wears no hat, his hair is long and sun-streaked. He pulls up a chair at a table across the room, turns it around and, like he's riding a horse, spreads his legs across and relaxes into the seat as if he has all the time in the world. Linda is riveted. She can't help it. His clear blue gaze lands on her. She hides behind her yellow pad, scribbling furiously.

What she writes: "Death Valley. Funeral Mountains. Did the early prospectors figure they could beat mortality to the punch with these macabre names? Devil's Cornfield, Bad Water Basin, Starvation Canyon, Coffin Peak. I don't have their morbid sense of humor. I write down these names and see decomposing bodies, desiccated tissue."

The man orders a beer, waits for it to come, slaps some money down, gives her another look, and departs. She stops writing. Outside the window, translucent blue moths flutter around a courtyard lamp. She can hear minute explosions as they immolate themselves on the hot yellow glass.

There is no light back at the campsite. The sky, a deep plushy black, is strewn with more stars than Linda has seen since she was here as a child, when, each night, having to pee, she'd climb out of the family tent to a spot where no one could see. Squatting, she'd look up at the Milky Way, smeared like chalk across a blackboard. She always forgot to bring toilet paper; she'd stay crouched, stargazing, letting the cold night air dry her.

Linda wishes she had a telescope. Daniel has one, from when he was interested in astronomy. She should have brought it. Found the planets. Examined nebulae and globulae, clusters, galaxies. Outer space is clean, she concludes. Vacuumed. No memories. No emotions. She qualifies — that's how it looks from earth, where you can't see the debris, the fragments of colliding meteors, the garbage from failed space shuttles, the dust which may or may not be the same stardust from which we all are made.

She pulls out a tarp and a fiber-filled sleeping bag, one of three she and Daniel purchased for emergencies after a major earthquake. Imitating her father, she paces the site, scrutinizing the terrain for the most level, and least rocky, area.

Is Sam asleep, she wonders, or is he waiting for her to come kiss him good night?

When she is able to speak, when she can resume her role as mother-protector, she'll bring him camping.

She spreads out the tarp, unfurls the sleeping bag, and then heads for the bathroom. Although there are a few vans, the only camper to brave the elements is the man with the long hair she'd seen in the saloon. He seems to be juggling light-sticks in the dark, although he probably is positioning them, so he doesn't trip on his campsite clutter. He doesn't notice her.

In the middle of the night, Linda awakens. Disoriented, she reaches for Daniel. He's not there. Her bedroom has vanished. She has to pee. She can't ignore it. She wriggles out of her sleeping bag cocoon. The cold pierces her heart, cold like the dark side of the moon. She stuffs her fist in her mouth, otherwise she accidentally might make a sound and ruin her vocal cords forever. She has forgotten that she's on a Hero's Journey.

Stumbling to a gully, she squats, the way she did as a child, and releases a hot stream of urine. Too late she recalls that it rarely rains here, that whatever mark her urine produces could be imprinted in the topsoil for years, becoming part of the geological inventory. Unless there's a dust storm. A ferocious dust storm, toppling tents, moving trailers, etching car windows, erasing the landscape... but not now, please. Not while she turns her face to the sky, transfixed by the stars, by the infinite dimension of the universe.

# 24. Desolation canyon

Linda removes her wedding ring. She rationalizes her fingers will swell up in the heat of the day and she'll be more comfortable. The gold band is deposited in the glove compartment of her car, which she locks. Her hand is lighter, unencumbered. She flutters it through the air, amazed and guilty that she, herself, has become more buoyant.

Linda drives to the trailhead of an arid black rock canyon, home to hawks, buzzards, and the infrequent big horn sheep. She has nothing in mind except to walk.

The alluvium — gritty sand from centuries of erosion — crunches under her feet as she enters the mouth of the canyon.

Why are entrances to canyons always called mouths, as if the hiker is a food particle to be ingested?

This is our question, not hers. She concentrates on her stride — long loose steps, her arms swinging, a water bottle bouncing against her hip.

The landscape is harsh. The average rainfall at Furnace Creek is only 1.66 inches a year. High temperatures and low humidity account for the intense evaporation rate of any rain that does manage to push itself past the mountains. You can look up these statistics. What little vegetation there is, scrubby growth, parched lichen, clings to life with a dogged stubbornness that Linda tries to appreciate, but finds herself resenting, as if the triumph of organic matter in the face of all odds is a judgment against her.

"Spoiled softy," the dry sticks accuse. "All you have to do to get water is turn on a faucet."

She rubs her naked ring finger. The strip of white skin has begun to turn pink. She picks up the pace. If she walks long and hard enough, endorphins will take over, and she'll be in the moment, wherever that is. Her breath quickens; sweat streaks her sunscreen, stinging her eyes. She pauses.

Walls loom on either side. Horizontal layers across their face testify to the rise and demise of epochs. The roar of volcanic eruptions, the reverberation of shifting tectonic plates, the sibilant drying of inland seas, the screams of animals on their way to extinction — all articulated soundlessly in stone.

She keeps going. The canyon narrows, darkens. She shudders. Perhaps it will swallow her. She stops and reaches out to touch the sides of hardened magma, of basalt threaded with granite. High above, the sky is a thin blue line. A lizard crawls up a steep fissure towards the sun; without thinking, she follows, up and up and up.

When Linda was a little girl, she was not afraid of heights, and never hesitated to shimmy to the top of trees or climb out on precipices. She was the one parents sent to assist their stranded children down from scary places.

Linda is not a little girl. She is a grown woman whose husband and son have no idea that she is scaling the sheer side of a cliff. Nor does anyone else.

The lizard vanishes. Linda is not a rock climber; she has no ropes or pitons. There are no ridges for her fingers to grip. It is impossible to continue. She looks down at her shoes. They are planted precariously on a narrow shelf high above the canyon floor, with no place to go. She stops breathing. Buzzards circle overhead.

She is stuck. This is a crisis of her own making. No menacing psychopath chased her; no literary device arbitrarily cornered her.

The buzzards are patient. They will circle as long as it takes, then make off with the carrion she will become if she doesn't take a breath, drink some water and figure out a way back down.

She lifts her water bottle. The movement upends shards of rock, which plummet off the side. When at last their echo dies away, she very slowly sips the water. Otherwise, she doesn't move.

Back at the campground, the man with the long hair ambles over to her site, curious about the red stiletto heels on top of a yellow pad on the picnic table, about the woman who wears them — where she is, and why he hasn't seen her. He can't envision that she's hanging off the side of a cliff. But if he could envision it, if we allowed him to, what would he do? Jump into his jeep, race through the canyon, scale the wall, and carry her out piggyback? Or would he have us skip ahead to a terrifying free-fall where, unable to catch her, he can do nothing except watch helplessly, and replay the image in the dark of his mind, his own catastrophic snuff film?

Linda stares down at the canyon floor, hoping a ranger will come. She has always liked rangers, in their olive-green uniforms with their enthusiasm for nature and their expertise regarding trail safety and dehydration and rescue operations. She expects that the ranger will have seen her car and be on the lookout for her.

But how will she attract attention? She can't cry out. She is forbidden to make a sound, no matter what the provocation. If she throws a rock, she might destabilize her narrow shelf, and, like the shards, moments ago, plummet off the precipitous drop to certain death.

Then what? Her little boy, motherless. She never even said 'good-bye,' just a hasty note on the refrigerator door. Plus, there is the great probability, no, make that a certainty, that Daniel will get over the loss and remarry, providing Sam with a newer, better mother. Sam, left with no actual photos of his original mom, except the ones she's given him of Will and Without Will, because everything else is digital and subject to deletion. How quickly will she be forgotten? A tasty coq au vin. This unfinished novel. How much weight does her life hold?

Linda wishes she were a lizard. She wishes she could climb vertical walls and shed her skin and if she lost a tail, she could grow another. Her eyes fill with tears again. Why do these tears keep happening? Maybe she is a lizard, a human lizard, sloughing off one identity for another, undergoing a kind of death, stuck on the ridge unable to move. Maybe there's a real death on its way. Buzzards know; that's why they won't leave.

If she had a voice, she could shout at them to go away.

That's not true. Before the surgery, she couldn't shout; she couldn't even summon a bored waiter in an empty restaurant. They never heard her, while Daniel could catch their attention with nothing more than a slight cough, or a quiet, "Excuse me". One of Linda's squeaks would not have scared off the buzzards. Quite the opposite, such a helpless sound would have attracted them.

A hawk swoops by, keen eyes fixed on smaller prey.

There will be no rescue.

Tears won't get her off the rocks. She has to retrace

her steps. But backwards is not the same as forwards. She can't look where she's going without upsetting her body's precarious balance. There's a chance she'll stumble or slip in an avalanche of scree. She has to go blindly. She has to trust. She curses herself for not remembering to carry a whistle, although there is no ranger, nor other hikers in Desolation Canyon, the name of this place. That's what it is. That's what she is. Desolate and about to die.

## 25. Meanwhile...

Daniel bops Sam on the head with a brand-new junior tennis racquet.

"This is for you, kidlet."

They go to the public courts in Griffith Park and Daniel gives his son his first tennis lesson.

"We'll surprise Mom," he encourages, lobbing a slow ball across the net, "and show her what fun it is."

Sam enjoys hitting the ball back to his father. So long as he doesn't have to run all over the place for it.

"I'm saving my legs for soccer," he explains.

Daniel wants to scoop him up and throw him in the air and whirl him around like an airplane. He's flooded with love. Though he never would have initiated it, he's grateful that Linda has given them this time alone. Usually, his experience of Sam is filtered through Linda, who always wants him to interact more, but doesn't allow for the opportunity.

Does he miss her?

Honestly?

He's not sure. He aches for Rosie, but Linda?

# 26. Woman in the dunes

Linda made it out of Desolation Canyon. Paralysis was not an option. Clinging to the steep wall, she inched her way down, going nose to nose with layers of volcanic rock, with fossils of mollusks and ancient fish, with slashes of rose quartz that resembled scar tissue surrounded by streaks of black obsidian. When at last she reached the bottom, though she longed to drop to her knees and weep with relief, flies swarmed all over her, their buzzing so intense she found herself running away from them through the noon blaze on the canyon floor, through the white heat generated by the dark stone, running until her legs buckled. Then the flies attacked, like the Furies in an ancient Greek production of Aeschylus' tragic trilogy, Oresteia. She was being punished for a crime she couldn't recall committing.

## AN INTERLUDE
## WHILE LINDA RESETS HER EQUILIBRIUM

The Furies didn't follow her into the car. She is alive. She is safe. She rewards herself by indulging in a brief recess, an authorial meander away from the exploration of canyons and the inherent risk of her hero's journey. She cossets herself with sand dunes. From a distance, they resemble melting scoops of vanilla ice cream. Up close, sitting at the base of one, a thin stream of sand slipping through her fingers, she can see the world in a single grain. An image in a poem she read. She doesn't remember more than that. Nor does she care. (If you do, it's from a poem by William Blake: "To see a world in a grain of sand/ And a heaven in a wild flower, / Hold infinity in the palm of your hand / And eternity in an hour.") Linda is grateful, grateful for the warm surface beneath her body, grateful to be in one piece.

Unable to shout for joy, forbidden to vocalize in any way, she opts for physical expression. This is new for her. She is not a dancer, like Marta of the Amargosa Opera House, nor an athlete, nor has she ever used her hands in the Mediterranean fashion to punctuate intention. Until now, if emotions weren't clarified by words, she wasn't sure they were real. She takes off her hiking boots and socks, scrambles to the top of the dune where she stretches her arms to the sun overhead. She shuts her eyes and glues her mouth tight to keep out the sand, and then falls, deliberately, the way she did when she was young, rolling faster and faster, dizzy and out of control, very much alive.

She lies nears the bottom, splayed out like a blissful fallen angel, a dusting of sand on her eyebrows and between her toes, unaware that two dunes over, the man with the long hair and the loping walk has assumed a similar position, shirt off, dark glasses on, asleep, soaking up the rays.

A foreign tourist, one of many thousands of visitors, snaps a photo of Linda. He will download it when he gets back to Furnace Creek Inn where his tour group is staying, and on his blog, her image will appear with a Japanese title: Suna no Onna — Woman in the Dunes.

### INTERLUDE IS OVER

Revived, Linda eats an orange, and heads for a different canyon, one with a more promising name: Golden Canyon.

She was here as a child, prevented from exploring alone by her parents who were afraid she might get lost. Now she is an adult with no one to place limits on her. She can go where she wants. She can lose herself amidst the carved rocks, the labyrinths of Georgia O'Keefe sculpted shapes. She can lose herself, and then find herself — she has all the time in the world.

Golden Canyon catches the glint of the sun. She is walking through radiance.

Drawn by a tributary off to the side, she abandons the main trail. The air is still. The spongy earth muffles any sound. There are no birdcalls, no vibrations from distant automobiles. There are no human voices. She is liberated by the silence. Amplified by the silence. Unlike those of us who speak out loud, dropping phrases into the air, littering the quiet with careless sentences, Linda has become part of the ecology.

If we were to be faithful to her reality, the paragraph would read:

But this is a narrative, a report, a chronicle, a recounting of events, which may or may not be occurring.

Linda's reality is not the only one. There is the author's reality, the reader's reality. Empty pages could be construed to mean anything. Un-fabricated, full of potential. A newborn minus its genetic map. Not a novel.

For once, Linda is not thinking about empty pages.

She mounts curves of mute sandstone, this time without fear. Even if she fell, she couldn't be hurt. The scale is gentle, rounded, a soft mother of earth drawing her into its folds, urging her into its reservoir of stillness. She is released from inhibition.

At the perfect vantage point — a secluded cleft in the pink sandstone, beneath sculpted spirals — Linda waits for the sun to shift. She waits on her back, her shirt off, her jeans and underpants pulled down, her skin exposed. She feels the air, the support of the earth.

Minutes pass.

A ray slants over the sandstone wall, dispersing shadow.

Bemused by her own suspension of disbelief, dazzled by beams and shafts of light, she wills them into her vagina, spread open with her fingers. There is no wound, no Freudian mutilation to scare off faint-hearted husbands. There is only healthy tissue.

Her hips lift. Her finger moves in a primal dance with her designated sun-god-lover. This is no longer a contrivance, no longer a hypothetical exercise in animism. Eyes closed, she gives over to the experience. Her body rocks harder, faster. As she climaxes, she is filled with a powerful brilliance in which boundaries vanish, and the earth and sun fuse into liquid gold melting through her veins, and when, at their next and final session, she is asked by Faith whether she felt transformed, she will say, that for one moment, at least, yes, she did.

On her way back to the car, pants zipped, shirt buttoned, she passes a group of hikers led by a park ranger in an olive uniform. They all look at her. The ranger tips his hat. She waves to them. They wave back.

Do they know? Could they have seen? Brushing yellow dust and specks of pink off her arms and out of her hair, Linda embraces her audacity.

Naked in public, fucking the sun!

He comes to Linda while she is in the saloon. She's eating appetizers, assorted and unappealing. He puts his hand over hers. The heat radiating from his palm jolts her. She withdraws her hand and looks up, into endless sky-blue eyes.

"The mystery woman." A smile, like a Technicolor song. "Do you have any idea how sexy a pair of red high heels on a campsite table can be?"

She is glad she can't talk, because she has no idea what she'd say.

He looks at her appetizers. "Why don't you let me cook dinner for you?" he asks. "I've got something a lot better than this back at camp."

Although curious about what he would serve, she shakes her head.

He moves her yellow pad so he can read what's there: "The salt flats, the lava, the dunes — everything absorbs sound. The beating of a heart can be overwhelming."

He nods in agreement. "That's the thing about this place. We find our heartbeat."

His hand goes back on hers. There is a woven band around his wrist, red and orange, the ends frayed, probably crafted by some indigenous artisan in a depleted rain forest. It rests right next to a watch—the high-tech kind that remembers phone numbers and dates and predicts the weather and reads your pulse. She wonders if the watch is registering a change in his pulse, or hers. She wonders if it knows what the weather is like in Los Angeles, and whether Sam will play in his soccer game and whether Daniel is worried that she is meeting this man with long hair and sky-blue eyes, who looks like a cowboy, yet adorns his wrist with a frayed indigenous bracelet and a space-age time-piece.

"You must be a writer," the man observes, his gaze embracing the yellow pad.

The validation is a balm.

"Come on," he urges. "I'll make stir-fry, with fresh ginger. We can discuss words."

She cocks her head, allowing the hand to stay where it is. She enjoys its warm energy, how it flows right into her skin, like the sun.

"Whatever words you like. Or we can discuss where you've been all day."

Had he known she was stranded on a cliff, he would've tried to rescue her, she's positive.

Her silence mystifies him. "Do you understand what I'm saying?"

Using her free hand, she peels off a clean sheet of paper.

"Yes," she writes, but she does not offer the reason for her silence.

He takes the pen from her, and prints in letters that slant backwards, "Good." He looks happy, as if they've made a beginning. "Who are you?" he adds, the capital W shaded, as if he were an artist.

That question.

She is tempted to create a new character. I am Edna, from a small Russian village that disappeared because of climate change. I am Francesca, a poet whose work is so oblique, not even I comprehend it. She removes the pen from his hand. The plastic retains his warmth. Will she put down the name she wishes she'd chosen in the beginning —Simone — and see where destiny leads?

He waits, curious.

"No names," she writes, instead.

Deciding to play her game, if that's what it is, he doesn't know, but she's captured his attention, he lifts a pencil off the waitress' tray, a short stubby No. 2 with a chipped yellow surface. He uses script now, looping letters, easy to read. "I don't believe in names, either. I believe in choices." The lead smears a little, from the heel of his hand pressing down.

"A name can be a choice," she scribbles rapidly, enjoying this exchange, the kind she wants with Daniel, who never has the patience for it.

"Choose to have dinner with me," he scrawls.

She glances at her stale nachos and the pickles, the greasy fried zucchini, and decides.

Later, she'll ask how he knew she belonged to the red shoes.

His campsite is a cacophony of color — vividly striped rugs, silver mylar space blankets, orange and chartreuse pillows, gleaming lemons and avocados piled high in a cobalt pot, ropes of bright red chilis drying in the desert air. The strains of a gamelon, or a synthesizer, or Tuva throat singers gravitate from an old fashioned boombox next to a pile of techno CDs, electronic riffs co-opted from tribal melodies. She's in the nest of a rave deejay, a cyber vagabond. He invites her to recline on a cushion. She hesitates. Reclining means trust, vulnerability. Her yellow pad is clutched to her chest, covering her breasts.

He does have a wok. He has sharp knives and fresh vegetables and aromatic spices and a small bottle of cold-pressed extra-virgin olive oil. She fingers the label — an Italian peasant girl with a jar of oil resting on one voluptuous hip. That must be the virgin. How can something be 'extra' virgin?

Her host smokes a joint while he cooks, and although she refuses to join him, the air is heavy with scent, and she finds herself reclining, after all, her head settled against a pillow, and she becomes fascinated by the butane flames. Blue. Green. Pixels of color transmuting into kaleidoscopic graphics.

"I haven't been with a woman for a long time," he tells her, while spooning the first course into a light-as-air titanium backpacking bowl from which they both will eat.

Does he mean 'with' in the biblical sense, or 'with,' as being in the company of? The yellow pad has fallen to the ground; she has no intention of reaching for it.

"I've been in the Andes, studying Peruvian Mountain flutes."

Zamponas, Antaras, Quenas. These words mean nothing to her. Nor do they determine what kind of 'with' he means. She lets his explanations lap against her brain like quiet surf. It isn't until he takes out a bamboo pipe and begins to play that she understands.

She doesn't know this man. She doesn't know his name, or what he does for a living. But after listening to the first few plaintive notes, her throat closes up and the tears begin and she fears that 'with' goes deeper, further than she's ever been, or is willing to go. These simple hollow reeds, used by Pan and the ancient Greeks, produce a sound so mesmerizing it's no wonder the satyrs were able to lure respectable women into their randy clutches.

She knows she should flee, but she has tasted the food, and after a day of hiking and only oranges and bad appetizers to eat, she can't resist one more bite.

He puts the instrument down.

"Wow. I've never seen anyone cry without making any

noise." He wipes away one of her tears. "There's a perfect stillness about you that Tibetan monks meditating an entire lifetime would envy."

He kisses her.

Linda has not had sex with anyone but Daniel since she's been married. Before Daniel, there'd been a few fleeting affairs, one minor relationship, nothing much, unless you count an evening in the East Village during her New York summer when an art student had taken her to his fourth floor walk-up, stripped, climbed on a chair, and with an erect, discolored penis, posed as the crucified Jesus until finally she asked him to come off the cross.

She's a married woman now, but this man doesn't know that; she's not wearing a wedding ring.

The temperature drops; she didn't bring a sweater. He wraps his arms around her. The rhythm of the mountain flute continues in the soft push of his lips against hers, as he presses and releases, presses and releases, so that her lips become part of the song. This man, his long hair caressing her shoulders, asks no questions about her muteness, accepting her as she is, a mystery woman with red stiletto heels on a campsite table and an appetite for stir-fry.

She touches his chest, still warm from the sun's rays. He feels different from Daniel, smoother, younger. She feels different in his hands. He is massaging her. Tension evaporates. Forgetting to hold fast, her muscles submit to his touch. He lingers over her breasts. They glow white against his tan. Rippling, circular movements, around and around. They are no longer breasts. They are pools of erotic sensation. How did he learn to do this? Another Andes secret? Not even when she nursed Sam did her breasts provide this pleasure. He smiles down at her. She blushes, unwilling for him to see how much she's enjoying this.

"It's okay," he whispers. "We've got all night."

And then what? Will he disappear at the first light, fly away like those immortal deities who assume their male-ness only in the cloak of dark?

She pulls his head back to hers, her tongue, unshack-led, reaching into his mouth, hungry for his breath. Inhala-tion, exhalation. Oxygen and prana. His breath prompting her own.

Her thighs glide apart. He relaxes onto her body, which has been divested of covering, she can't remember how; barriers seem to have evanesced. Down deep, the root of her spine, in some dormant chakra, there is a power-ful awakening. As if the gods have lit a fire. She extends, opens, dilates; she is a current as he slides inside her. Their rhythm intensifies. His hands pin her arms back, over her head. She strains against him, and her arousal becomes more acute. Definitions drop away. Wife, mother, post-op patient. She is heat and desire, a partner in the music.

He moves his hands down her arms. His palms caress her armpits, her chest. His fingers encircle her throat. Her throat. His thumbs begin to press and then release, and then press harder.

Not her throat.

He manipulates the blood-flow, making her head spin.

Not her throat.

She's having sex with a stranger in the desert under a mantle of stars and he could press down on her wind-pipe and choke her and no one would know. His thrusts are deeper, faster, and, even as she shakes her head, 'no,' her vaginal walls spasm, and her body writhes. Everything turns red, whirling out of control. She shakes her head more violently: 'No, no, no!' He doesn't notice, or he thinks it's passion, or he doesn't care because he isn't a rave deejay or a cyber-vagabond, he's a serial killer who hasn't been with a woman in a long time because he's strangled them all. She can't scream.

Linda can't scream. That's a fact. Even if, in order to save her life, she disobeyed the doctor's orders, she still couldn't scream. Her vocal cord would not create a sound. She has no voice at all.

He gazes down at her, a soft serious expression on his face, his thumbs relaxed. Heart racing, she angles her elbows between his arms in a long-forgotten karate move from a self-defense class she once took with Stephanie, and whacks his hands away from her neck. She tries to punch his chin, but he catches her wrist.

"I thought you liked it," he whispers.

To mix sex with death?

Her body is shaking.

"It wasn't to hurt you, but to give you pleasure."

He's lying.

"I'd never hurt you."

He means it.

She begins gathering her clothes, flung on cushions like confetti from a New Year's Eve party gone sour.

"There's no reason to be afraid."

He sits on his heels, a monk in prayer.

To pray. To prey. Why do they sound the same?

"Don't go."

She returns to her campsite where, gripping an extra-long Maglite flashlight, almost as long as a bat and just as heavy, she lies awake all night, watching the stars move much too slowly across the horizon. Her body continues to shake, not in fear, nor trepidation that he will seek her out again, although she's prepared if he does, but in visceral reaction to its own pitched sexual experience. She's been turned inside out. She fingers her neck. She's read about teen-age boys who accidentally hang themselves in the midst of an autoerotic experience. She remembers the end of Melville's Billy Budd — how the sailors knew Billy climaxed at the moment the noose tightened. But even if the stranger had been trying to intensify her pleasure, and she accepts that might have been the case, he crossed over the line. Who did he think she was?

She goes to her car, and, using the flashlight, examines her throat in the rear-view mirror. There are no bruises.

He didn't force her to be with him. She chose to be. That's why she's shaking.

She, Linda Gregory, crossed over a line.

As soon as the sky lightens, she takes her yellow pad and the flashlight across the campground, not noticing that her feet are bare or that she has no underpants on beneath the T-shirt. She finds him asleep on cushions, covered by a space blanket. The flutes, lined up like toy soldiers, stand guard. Without disturbing them, the Maglite handy in case, she lies next to him so quietly he barely realizes that he's not in a dream state, and she reaches down under the blanket, resisting the impulse to grab his cock, twist it, strangle its blood supply; instead, she seeks retaliation—or maybe resolution, or a redressing of power — by touching it softly, finger wings drifting across his skin, until it stirs.

She moves away, and by the time he opens his eyes, the only evidence she was there is the absence of a Peruvian flute from the middle of the line-up— a small one with a feather dangling — and a sheet of paper on which is written: "How did you know the red shoes were mine?"

# 28. Acting out

Sam is going through a rough patch. He doesn't want to play in the soccer game unless his mother comes, too. Daniel tries to explain that Linda is on little trip.

"Why?" wails Sam.

Daniel says sometimes mothers need breaks.

"But she was just in the hospital."

"That's not really a break," answers Daniel.

Sam thinks it's his fault. He wasn't quiet enough, and so he hurt her throat, and so she doesn't love him anymore.

Daniel says that's not true.

Sam doesn't believe him.

## 29. The waters

Hot springs sit outside the park boundaries in kind of a no-man-or-woman's land dotted with tumbleweed. Barely indicated by a metal sign, pellet pocked and twisted, the painted letters unreadable, a structure squats low on gravelly soil, its cement block masonry a buttress against fierce windstorms that hurl unimpeded across the desert.

This is the place Linda finds on a map, a mere dot off a single lane highway. She is compelled by a need to immerse herself in water, to wash away the dust and the taste and smell of sex before she returns home. Jews have mikvahs for purification; Christians, lavers and holy water; Hindus, the Ganges; Muslims, their rituals of wudu or ghusi. Here is where she has chosen to cleanse her body if not her spirit.

She steps into what passes for an office and a changing area. There is a modest fee. This is no spa. Spas have soothing music and essential oil aromatherapies perfuming the atmosphere. The air here reeks of rotten eggs, the smell of sulfur. Amenities are minimal: a few bent nail hooks, some splintery shelves, rust-streaked toilets, one shower head, a drinking fountain that spews metallic tasting liquid. Chain link surrounds the outside pools. Cracked corrugated panels are the sole source of shade. Not a promising location for symbolic ablutions.

She dons her bathing suit. She takes the requisite shower and makes her way to the pools. The cement is warm on her bare feet. She stops.

In unison, faces turn to peer at her. Linda is at least three decades younger than the youngest of them. She blinks. Can she be seeing correctly? Are they the living dead, ravenous for fresh meat, licking dry, flaky lips in anticipation? Stuff of horror movies she and Daniel used to watch. Not just her age, her bathing suit sets her apart. Without exception, they are naked.

"Where did you descend from?" the question floats towards her.

Linda shakes off visions of zombies and dips a toe in one of the pools.

"Not in there!" shouts a superannuated denizen, his walker near-by.

Her toe jerks backward.

"It's too hot. You need to adjust first."

"How do you know what's too hot for her? Just because you have high blood pressure," responds a woman whose varicose veins stand out like trails of a well-used lifetime. "Go on, dear, it won't cook you."

"In fact, whatever ails you, the sulfur water's good for it," adds another lady smearing her generous flesh with cocoa butter. "That's why we have our Senior Access bus take us here once a week. We belong to the Pahrump Arthritis Sufferers Club, sufferer pronounced 'sulfurer.'"

A tiny shriveled peanut speaks up. "Ms. Know-know-it-all, tell her why sulfur goes hand in forked tail with Satan."

"Uh, oh, here comes the lecture," predicts a man in a different pool, his vulnerable pate shielded by a well-worn Chicago Cubs cap.

The tiny woman stands on a step so Linda will be sure to hear. "She won't tell you. But I will. Sulfur is the same thing as brimstone. That is to say, it's a stone found on the brim of volcanic craters. Exhumed from the molten heat of hell, Satan's domain." For emphasis she tosses long wild tresses, gray, with streaks of black, and split ends. Her pointy chin and hooked beak give her a witchy cast.

"When the good book says it rained fire and brimstone, it is referring to an eruption of a volcano."

Steam curls out of one of the vents.

The cocoa butter lady slaps her thigh, hooting, "I guess we're a bunch of sinners dancing the day away with the tune of Satan's sulfur in our noses."

"Ah, sin," sighs the man with the walker. "I would if I could."

Linda smiles. These aren't feral seniors waiting to pounce on her. They're just retirees from Pahrump, a town on the Nevada side, having a good time. She puts one whole foot into the hottest pool, and then the other. While she adjusts to the temperature, the peanut of a woman introduces herself.

"I'm Margareta. And you are?"

Linda prints her name in water on the cement.

"I wouldn't have guessed you as a Linda—"

Her name disappears, the letters evaporating in the hot dry air.

"Not a Linda," echoes Chicago Cub hat. "Definitely not."

"You're a brave woman to risk coming into this particular pool." Margareta flashes a defiant look at the others. "They don't approve of me."

"Don't be spouting any of your rubbish!" warns the varicose veined lady. "Linda is a young and beautiful girl who doesn't want to talk out loud to us." Eyeing her, "And she's just had her own hot time in the old town last night, I'll bet my bottom dollar."

Mortified, Linda dunks under the water.

Who are these people? She no longer considers them benign. Is the arthritis club some sort of coven?

She holds her breath for as long as she can. When she emerges, hair dripping, she ignores them. She finds a seat near a jet, sits, closes her eyes, and while soaking in the hot mineral pool, waiting for her body to expel its toxins, she tilts her head to the sky.

That lady could tell she'd had sex. Is it that obvious? Will Daniel know? When they make love again, if they ever do, will he see the sun-surfing stranger hovering in her head, a man who lavished more physical attention on her body than she'd thought possible, even if conceivably he did try to kill her?

She places her hands on her throat. How little pressure it would have taken to extinguish her life.

He must have awakened by now, climbed out from under that mylar space blanket, checked his campsite and discovered that she had re-visited before he awakened, that she wasn't scared of him after all, that she was the reason for his early morning erection. And that she had stolen one of his flutes.

Linda is glad that she never learned his name, or who or what he really was.

What about us? We readers desire details; we are insatiable in our hunger to 'know.' Would our perception of him change if he's described as an annuity salesman from Bakersfield who sold enough policies to pay for a trip to Peru, and that on his return, before nestling into his cubicle and hustling more sales, he veered east to chill in the sun on Death Valley's dunes? Or conversely if we're told he is born of old-world royalty, a trust baby on the run from rabid fortune hunters? Do we gain anything if it is posited that one day, trolling the net, he'll discover a photo, Suna no Onna — Woman in the Dunes — which he will print out and frame because he recognizes the nameless woman in the photograph and he can still feel the way her silence touched his heart?

Now that she's safe, while she soaks in the hot springs, let's honor Linda's version, the one she prefers: a stranger who appeared from nowhere as if he were Apollo, or another sun-deity incarnate.

Which leaves her to ponder two questions:

1.Had she spent the night with him, would she have been rewarded with immortality?

2.Was she a coward for fleeing?

Margareta cocks her head, sensing more to this woman than voicelessness.

The water does its job. Linda relaxes. With effort she hoists herself out of the steaming pool and moves to a cooler one. She runs fingers through wet hair, revived.

No need for immortality. Being mortal suits her.

Margareta follows her, wading through the pool, using her hands like fins. With a bark like a seal, she gives Linda a tube. "Don't forget sunscreen."

The old woman's skin is so brown and wrinkled, Linda can't tell her age, or even her decade. She wonders if it's true that as females lose sexual value in the eyes of society, they are free to be more assertive. This disturbs her. She does not wish to believe that the authority of a female voice is connected to the absence of fecundity.

She applies sunscreen.

"Did you find in the desert what you came for?" Margareta asks.

Should she have stayed celibate, fasted and chased visions? Is she more who she is because her body challenged safety, because she climbed higher than she ought, because she dared to be penetrated, traversing the fine line between abandon and annihilation, not only with nature, but with man?

Will Daniel accuse her of being unfaithful? Does she

want him to?

She floats face down in the water. When she lifts her head up, Margareta is hovering over her.

"Were you camping, Linda? I once camped. I remember the howling of the wolves and diving into icy rivers, and screwing the pants off Freddie, the sax player at the Blue Note." Eyes tear up, remembering Freddie. "I was always drawn to the moon, the full harvest moon, the hunter moon, the super moon, the wolf moon, the blood moon. I half-expected to give birth to moon-babies; instead I gave birth to a brood of dysfunctional ungrateful slackers who never call," chuckling without self-pity, "except to ask for money."

She studies Linda, pats her arm.

"No moon-babies for you. You've been kissed by the sun."

Though Margareta's lips are chapped, and fold in where teeth should be, and her neck muscles are stringy and knotted, spirit animates her. Her black button eyes are full of life. Linda can't help but like her.

"Yes,' she marks in water on the cement. "I have."

There is no hurry to get home. She wonders what will be different between her and Daniel. And Sam. Will he have missed her? She hasn't hugged his perpetually-in-motion small body for three days. Still, she drives in the slow lane, sticking to the speed limit the entire way, savoring this new sense of herself. The explorer. The adventuress. The canyon climber. The god fornicator. The woman who slept with a stranger under the stars and survived.

She refuels in Barstow where she walks to the perimeter of the gas station. Shading her eyes, she looks out. The desert is there, a trace, visible beyond franchise restaurants and local industry, the silent landscape that she had entered.

Entering the landscape. That, she would tell Faith, was the accomplishment.

She takes out the mountain flute and blows through one of the openings. A soft windy sound emerges. She smiles. She might not be able to speak, but she can make herself heard. She'll be like the humpback whales she saw on the nature show, serenading an unseen audience deep in the blue-black sea, returning again and again for haunting encores.

# 30. The return

Daniel opens the door. Linda is wearing a light cotton sundress, a straw hat she bought at the hot springs, and her red stiletto heels. There's a glow to her skin — beyond the reach of UVA/UVB inhibitors. Are more subtle differences apparent? A change in the way she holds her shoulders or tosses the backpack to the floor?

Daniel doesn't consider himself an animal; he's never identified with bull elephants protecting their turf, or bucks in mating season locking antlers; nor was he ever swayed by the man-as-aggressive-ape theory spawned by such once-popular books as The Territorial Imperative — and yet, before Linda has put the sunglasses back in her purse, he rushes her to the living room where, avoiding the couch which is strewn with action figures and Lego blocks, he thrusts her down on the kidney-shaped coffee table, screwing her through her underpants.

When he's finished, he seems as startled by his behavior as she is.

"I guess Sam wasn't the only one who couldn't wait to see you," he sheepishly jokes, zipping up his fly.

Linda peels herself off the coffee table, uncertain as to what just occurred. It hadn't been unpleasant. Obviously, he was no longer bothered by the genitalia as wound thing. Over the years of their marriage, his sexual moves had become fairly predictable. For him to suddenly break out of the mold was gratifying. As if she rendered him wild.

Hands under her dress, she adjusts her panties.

Daniel smirks.

A smirk is difficult. We don't like smirks. There's a self-satisfaction to them that's alienating. But Daniel is smirking and there's nothing we can do about it. He has reclaimed his wife. From whom, from what, he has no idea. That's not part of his thinking. She went away; she needs to be reclaimed. Rosie doesn't enter the equation.

Linda checks her husband, to see if he's still rendered wild.

"Sam's at a soccer friend's house," he says, his demeanor reverting to Dad-in-charge.

Linda surveys the house. Clothes lying around. Dishes in the sink. Bread crusts on the counter. Lived in. Father-son time. Nothing to make her suspicious. No pink angora lint on the purple couch. Why should she be suspicious? Her husband, whose rejection sent her to Death Valley in the first place, has just consummated their relationship on the coffee table, catapulting Lego spaceships and People magazines onto the floor, so urgent was his desire.

She stares at the cover of the latest People. It features a femme fatale cougar starring in a popular nighttime series, her breasts thrust forward, her mouth beckoning, an object of desire designed to seduce the viewer's gaze. The truth sinks in. There was no desire. Daniel had to have her, but the urgency wasn't about desire.

She looks at him picking up the Legos, his long, lean frame bending gracefully, his shirt slightly damp from exertion. Where has his desire gone? When did it go? Is it really because she lost her voice? Or is that pure coincidence?

Linda knows the answer. No sense in avoiding it any longer. She knows because of her experience in the desert.

He met someone. The surgery, the wound, all of it, Daniel's pretext. A conveniently timed excuse. He was with someone in that funky bar, the one he lied about to Stephanie. Because, otherwise, he wouldn't have lied.

She's been a fool.

Daniel stands up. "Well, did the road trip work? Feel better? Not mad at me anymore?"

She removes the flute from her purse. She touches the feather, and then blows a few notes as she heads for the kitchen where she pours herself a very tall glass of cold water.

"What'd you do out in the desert?" Daniel trails after her.

She retrieves the iPad and starts to answer him.

"Never mind. I get the picture."

No, you don't, she thinks.

She types quickly, "When's Sam coming home?"

All of a sudden, he is yearning to be with Rosie.

Linda takes a quick shower, and goes to pick up Sam.

"I didn't miss you, Mom," her son says proudly, hurling his arms around her in a giant hug. "But I ate the candy anyway!"

On the way back to the house, Sam points to her left hand. "How come you're not wearing your wedding ring? Did you lose it?"

Chagrined — she'd completely forgotten she'd taken it off, and Daniel hadn't noticed — she removes the band from the glove compartment. Sam cups it in his hand like it's a magic ring from The Hobbit saga (which his dad started reading to him while Linda was gone) — the circle of his parents' union, his security, more precious than his new soccer uniform.

He places it on Linda's ring finger and smiles happily.

She feels a tightening, a constriction of her chest. She has to see Stephanie. The truth. Objective confirmation.

Stephanie and Linda have been confidantes since they shared diary pages in Junior High and wrote long letters in college. Now, it's e-mails. No truth ever has been too awful, no fantasy too bizarre to reveal, although the confessions usually are Stephanie's, on the order of I can't believe I went to Barney's and spent $10,000 on shoes I'll never wear because the salesman looked like Antonio Banderas and I was desperate for him to ask me out. Stephanie relishes her role of uninhibited single woman to Linda's domestic matron. For Linda, Stephanie is and always has been a touchstone, a reality base.

She waits until the next day, when Sam is at school and Daniel at work, after she's done the laundry, reluctantly washing out the dust and sand, the odors of sweat and sex and sulfur, all the remains of her journey because they might tempt her to return to the dunes and thus avoid the truth that looms at home.

Infatuation with Latin dancing has gobbled up Stephanie's decor. Her living room is a version of the Copacabana during America's mid-20th century mambo revolution, her dining room a street out of BUENA VISTA SOCIAL CLUB, every wall festooned with flyers and posters announcing evenings of Cha-Cha-Cha, Rhumba, Rueda, or Despelote, a hip-swiveling Cuban street dance. Stephanie double-spins up to Linda with a freshly made Margarita.

"I didn't have any fresh mint, or I would have made you a mojito, which, in case you weren't aware, was Hemingway's favorite drink."

Linda's tongue curls under the taste of lime and tequila. She whips out her yellow pad. "Forget Hemingway. You saw Daniel at that bar, didn't you?"

What does Stephanie say?

Is it ever a good idea to fuel suspicion about a friend's husband? Doesn't that kind of honesty turn around and bite you in the rear? She doesn't have much of a choice. Coming clean is built into the very definition of their life-long friendship.

"Was he with someone?" adds Linda.

"Out of context, I couldn't be sure."

"What context do you need? Either you saw him, or you didn't. This isn't a case of post-modern philosophy."

Stephanie laughs. She kisses her friend.

"Did you have a good time in Death Valley? How could you? How could anyone? Dirt, broken fingernails, brutal sun. You would've had more fun doing salsa."

She turns up the music and swivels Despelote style.

"If you'd just let me teach you, all your marital angst would disappear."

Linda has no stomach for a discourse on marital angst which Stephanie is capable of giving — Stephanie, who has never married, who believes men are like bagels, to be enjoyed but not counted on because there's always a hole.

Abruptly, she shuts off the music. Lively Caribbean posters hang silent. Only her pen makes noise, emphatic strokes on the yellow pad. Exclamation points. Underline.

"I want to know!!!"

Of course, Stephanie knows that Linda does not really want to know, what she wants is to be reassured.

"Tell me everything, and I'll let you teach me how to salsa. I promise."

Stephanie is stymied. She pushes at the cuticle of her thumb, a habit she's had since seventh grade.

Linda scribbles another sweetener. "We can give each other mani-pedis."

This Stephanie can't resist. They've been doing it since their first sleep-over way back when. She guides Linda to her enormous mirrored upstairs bathroom, where, from a vast array of colors, she selects Tropical Mango, her current favorite.

Linda picks Gunmetal Gray.

While they apply the colors to each other's toes, an answer ekes out, slowly, in a reluctant monotone.

"Daniel was in a corner booth."

"And..." prods Linda, printing with her left hand, keeping the applicator away from the paper.

Stephanie seems to have lost track of the story, focusing one hundred percent on Linda's toe nail, making sure the tiny brush strokes don't show.

Linda puts the applicator back in the bottle of Tropical Mango she's been applying to Stephanie's toes. She writes in large clear letters.

"With someone? Male? Female? Trans?"

"Female. Yes, I remember. I mean, she was hard to forget."

With that admission comes a slip of the hand. A slash of gun powder gray smears the top of Linda's foot. Stephanie's face caves. A wordless plea to Linda — don't make me say it.

"You remember more. You always do. Go on."

Silence. Stephanie grips Linda's foot as if it's a lifeline. She assiduously rubs the acrylic smear with non-toxic polish remover.

"I can take it. You should have seen me climbing cliffs in Death Valley."

Linda doesn't add anything about the sun, or the stranger.

A dramatic sigh. "Red hair. No. More like copper. I smiled at Daniel but he didn't see me." Stephanie pauses. "He was concentrating." Answering the unasked question, "Really concentrating."

So the polish will dry faster, she hands Linda a fan. It features Carmen Miranda under a hat made of fruit.

Linda holds her feet out. The nails are lined up in a row. She fans them furiously. Carmen Miranda loses her smile.

"Linda, I am so sorry!" Stephanie reaches out to touch her. "It could have been completely innocent — some actress he was interviewing for E-tainment."

Except he had lied.

Their nails dry. They go back downstairs.

Stephanie puts on the music. After a few swivels and with a forced cheeriness, she takes Linda's hand. "You promised."

The Latin beat begins. Linda surprises herself. By the conclusion of the obligatory salsa lesson, she has the moves down, executing crossover swivels, as well as outside and inside turns. The collapse she'd felt in her chest when she absorbed the fact that Daniel did not desire her, the punch in the gut at hearing Stephanie's words of confirmation, the shudder of self-contempt because she had ignored all along what was in front of her — those awful feelings haven't gone — but there is a joy to this Cuban music that is contagious. More than joy. An affirmation. She vibrates with the music of life. It won't last, of that she is sure, but right now, in the moment, dancing with her best friend, it permeates her body and that's okay.

## 31. Copper hair

Rosie is not a happy camper. Her singing career hasn't progressed beyond the Ground Bean. She doesn't have any new voice students, which means she has none. Mr. Gus Santini moved to Palms Springs with Miss Robin Luther accompanying him, and since then tips at the diner have been down. She blames Daniel.

Not that it's Daniel's fault. He didn't make Mr. Santini move.

She understands she must take responsibility for her own life. She fully believes, also, what goes around comes around. And she acknowledges some things are beyond her control; you have to 'let go and let God,' no matter how intensely you visualize. But none of it matters right now, because Daniel promised he'd help her, and he hasn't and if she hadn't met him she wouldn't have had expectations and she wouldn't be this disappointed.

It's more than that. She misses him. She misses spending time with him. The shift must have taken place when she was concentrating on career moves. Rosie is dumbfounded. She wants to be with him, even if he isn't able to help her.

The telephone sits there right next to the Mary Magdalene candle from the laundromat, an old-fashioned pink princess phone she bought at a garage sale. The pink princess warns her not to call. Vulnerability is not part of their agenda. The blessed Saint gazes upon her without judgment.

It's safe, Rosie argues. It's safe because Linda can't speak, therefore, she can't answer the phone. She wouldn't anyway. It's Daniel's cell phone. She dials.

What Rosie doesn't know is that the evening following the salsa dance lesson, while continuing to mull — 'mull' may not be the right word, obsess might be more accurate —over Stephanie's disclosure about her husband and the mystery woman at the bar, Linda rests on her marital bed snuggled next to Sam while they listen to Daniel read Lord of the Rings in a wonderfully dramatic voice. What Rosie doesn't know is that Linda has fucked a god, and she is not the squeaky mouse pushover she was before. What Rosie doesn't know is that Linda knows Daniel has strayed, cheated, betrayed, although she has yet to figure out what she will do with this knowledge.

Nor does Rosie know that Daniel's guilt feelings have multiplied since his wife's return from Death Valley. Perhaps something in Linda's attitude hints he is nearing the point past which there is no return and he despises himself for putting his family in jeopardy. Maybe he smelled the whiff of a stranger in the desert, and it scared him. Whatever the catalyst, Daniel has pledged, this very evening, to devote himself to being the best father and husband he can be.

His cell phone is unaware of his pledge. It's wedged between the pillows. Daniel lets it ring, but Sam, who loves any opportunity to handle an iPhone, immediately snatches it and answers.

"Hello. Who is this, please?"

He looks hurt.

"It's for Dad, but she won't say her name."

He hands it to Daniel who drops it like a hot potato as soon as he hears the voice.

Too late.

The anointed contralto sweeps past Daniel's ear to Linda's. She stares at the phone.

"Who was it?" asks Sam.

"Nobody," says his dad, flushing.

Rosie! Of course. Rosie with the copper hair.

Linda scrutinizes her toenails.

Sam wants Daniel to keep reading.

Linda sits up, turns so she can look directly at her husband.

Daniel tries to regain his composure.

Even though she cannot speak, and has yet to accuse him, he now knows she knows.

Rosie calls again. This time, Daniel says in an annoyed voice to cease calling, they aren't buying any subscriptions, and if he wanted one, he'd subscribe online.

Linda shifts her focus away from Daniel. She looks again at her painted toes. They resemble bullets. Ten little bullets.

Rosie slams down the pink princess receiver. Does Daniel think his wife is so stupid that she would believe a magazine solicitor called twice in a row? Could the man of her dreams be that dumb? Or is she, Rosie, so insignificant he can't be bothered to come up with a better brush-off? Rosie has never been so angry with anybody in her entire life, and, worst of all, there's no one she can talk to; her friends would tell her they told her so, getting involved with a married man means heartache and low self-esteem, a cliché version of the blues she's so good at singing.

If she wanted, she could leave threatening messages on his voicemail. She could tweet, smear his name across the internet, accuse him of sexual harassment; she could kidnap Sam and hold the child hostage in the meat locker at Joe's Diner until she got her record deal. Does Daniel appreciate the self-control she's using? No-o-o. He's not thinking about her at all. She should go over there, this very second, and denounce him in front of his wife and son. Linda is a decent person. She deserves to know what a cad her husband is.

Is there a gun in Rosie's closet? One that's not loaded, although somewhere else, tucked away, long forgotten, bullets are hidden? Can we imagine Rosie searching frantically through dozens of shoes until she finds a small metal box of ammo secured inside an Army-Navy surplus combat boot? Ten shiny bullets. All that's left from years ago, when, in a fit of paranoia — although as they say, if it's really happening, it's not paranoia — she had to get a restraining order, not for an abusive boyfriend, but for an angry and abusive neighbor who blamed her for the death of his cat because she'd once complained that it was killing birds and suggested he put a bell around its neck so the birds would know danger was near and fly away. When the restraining order didn't work, she visited a shooting range.

Rosie has never killed anything except mosquitoes; her plan of action does not see the whole picture: Daniel bleeding from multiple wounds; Linda hysterically calling 911, though, sadly, since she has no voice, the operator can't hear her plea for help. Nor does Rosie envision the trial, where she gets a life sentence for murder, and spends two decades on the inside, leading the prison women's choir all the way to a record deal, until finally she's paroled for good behavior, uncontested by Linda who figures that the singing teacher has paid her dues.

But that's the wrong story. It is not the one being written.

Rosie has no intention of killing, assaulting, or otherwise challenging Daniel. She doesn't own a pocket knife, let alone a gun.

Whose revenge fantasy are we reading then?

Linda's, of course. She no longer hears Daniel reciting the section about the giant Ents' attack on Isengard where the evil wizard resides. The efforts of those ancient trees are replaced by images of violent retribution against her straying husband. She is concocting a desperate convoluted attempt to punish him without having to confront him, herself.

It won't work, Linda, sorry. Rosie doesn't get to leap to the forefront, committing a crime of passion that's rooted in your distress.

Linda stares at her gunmetal toenails while Daniel clears his throat and continues to read. Sam is rapt as his father's voice fills the room.

With great effort, she raises her eyes away from her manicured feet and shifts the gaze to Daniel. It is a hard, unrelenting gaze that pierces through the recitation. He halts midway in a sentence, gripped by that gaze. J'accuse, it says. He can't respond.

What is a marriage worth?

# 32. The puzzle

Questions puzzling Linda:

#1. What is a marriage worth?

#2. What kind of people refuse to let their marriage go?

Instead of 'people' we'll say 'women.' We'll exclude those bound by religion, tradition, or economic circumstance. There have been women Linda regarded as ordinary sane human beings, who, when their marriage was rent asunder, turned into supercharged hellcats employing every trick in the book — ultimatums, seduction, tears, rages, blackmail, erotic massage, tantric sex, couple counseling, culinary delicacies, threats of suicide, of murder — all in the space of a week. She thinks of them as Hera, the ancient Greek Goddess of Marriage and Family, protecting a sacred bond, a prime mover in an epic tale where all is fair in love and war.

And then, there are other women whose tragic dramas are diminished by the endless litanies of blame recited over and over and over, by the mantle of persecuted victim they refuse to discard.

#3. Follow up to #2. Which type is Linda?

#4. If Rosie finds Daniel attractive, is he more attractive?

#5. Follow up to #4. Why does Rosie find Daniel attractive?

One answer is so obvious, it smothers the others, even the fact that her husband is an attractive man who is intelligent, funny, kind and enjoys life. He publishes E-tainment, with its fanbase of millions. His tweets go viral. He is among the people who can make and break careers. That's why he appeals to someone like Rosie.

#6. What does she mean, "someone like Rosie"?

Words that come to mind: Selfish Juvenile Slut Bitch Homewrecker.

She wishes she could scream them out loud in Rosie's ear using Daniel's cell phone to call her. She can't. She can't even moan them brokenly into her hands without permanently damaging her vocal cords.

The next day, the air between her and Daniel is charged. He waits for accusation. So consumed by anxious anticipation, he fails to notice that she is at sea, in shock. Her world is off kilter, color has vanished. All is gray. The green of the garden, a faded lifeless gray. Sound is muffled, distant voices in her ears. Spatial relationships shift. She smashes her head on cupboards, unaware they are there. When driving, she is in danger of losing her way, of sideswiping a parked SUV. Or hitting a squirrel. Or wrapping the car around the native oak in front of the neighbor's yard. Suspicions are one thing; actual knowledge is another.

Daniel waits, suspended. For the shoe to drop.

The red stiletto shoe that marked her space.

Gradually, she recognizes the world she is in, albeit different from before. Space returns to its normal geometry. The couch resumes its shade of purple. The bougainvillea its crimson.

She is not the same person she was before Death Valley, and so, when Sam is at a friend's home, and she and Daniel are alone, Linda takes out the yellow pad and writes a message to her husband.

Do not defend yourself. Do not apologize. Do not see Rosie again. Ever.

Daniel starts to speak.

She gives no quarter.

Determined to respond, determined to justify, he picks up her pencil.

Before he can make a mark, she yanks the pencil away. A new bright yellow Number 2, freshly sharpened. Keeping her eyes locked on his, she breaks it in half. A sliver of lead sticks out between the splintered wood.

## 33. A right to remain silent

Our need to talk is so pervasive, not only do we have programs devoted to talking, we have programs discussing those programs. Topics don't matter. We speak to hear ourselves speak. We prattle and tattle, babble and twaddle; we drivel, we quibble. We speak to elucidate, to obfuscate, to intimidate, to exaggerate, to procrastinate, to fascinate, to maintain, declare, warrant, and confess. Given the proper circumstances, we confess to anything.

The law recognizes our weakness and offers us the right to remain silent.

Linda affirms her right. She stops carrying an iPad or a yellow pad. Words have not become her enemy, but she no longer seeks them out.

Dr. Raven, if Linda paid a visit, might wonder out loud, in that sympathetic neutral voice so distinctly hers, whether the discovery of Daniel's infidelity catapulted her into a depression, if enclosing herself in silence was akin to burrowing under a comforter. The question would not be neutral. Nor would be her appraisal of Linda's silence.

Since its Viennese inception, Dr. Raven's profession has been known as the Talking Cure; it depends on patients communicating in words. Despite her appreciation for quiet activities such as gardening, Faith is chary of total silence. Diarrhea of the mouth, as her daughter once scorned it, presents one of the more challenging aspects of an analytic practice, but she much prefers too much talk to those persons — at least those in non-clinical situations — who sit back and say nothing. Faith finds them stingy, as if they're hoarding words. During her children's teenage years, the loaded pauses at dinner that stretched from soup to pudding gave her acute anxiety attacks. As far as Faith is concerned, silence equals death.

It's just as well that Linda doesn't see her during this period.

Instead she Googles 'silence', and comes across an article about Baba Hari Das, affectionately known as Babaji, a spiritual teacher who has not spoken for over seventeen years. His energy is so focused that when students ask him questions, he can channel the answers to his assistant who then speaks out loud. Linda thinks this might be apocryphal, but she does perceive that being unable to speak provides her with unexpected focus. She observes more, she hears between the lines, her thought process is less hurried, and when the family sits down for meals, instead of tracking chitchat — how was your day, what did you do in school, etc. — she concentrates fully on the taste and texture of the food.

Sam begins to copy her. He eats more slowly. He doesn't speak as much. If he has to show her something, instead of shouting "Mom!" at the top of his lungs, he goes up to her and takes her hand and leads her.

Daniel is affected. The quiet makes him antsy. He wants to get away from it. There is something creepy about a wife who says nothing but listens with such stillness that his own voice reverberates back as if it's coming over a loudspeaker. He wants to go to ball games where people shout and scream.

"Hey, you don't have to chew your food a thousand times, like some kind of cow," he tells Sam.

The boy's hurt expression shames him.

"Forget I said that. You'll live longer. I eat too fast." He starts chomping very slowly and deliberately. "See, I'm doing it too."

Sam giggles.

"You know what? You and I have to take in a Laker game one of these days."

That gets Sam out of the chair, screeching with excitement. Daniel finds the audible commotion inordinately gratifying.

Linda counts the flavors exploding out of a forkful of brown rice. It's as though she's never really eaten before.

There is a website she found — LE CENTRE DU SILENCE. On it she read: "In the beginning was the word, before the word there was movement, before movement there was silence."

Satisfied that Sam can still screech and holler, Daniel attempts a conversation with Linda. "We're doing a piece about past hosts of the Academy Awards. We're polling our readers for their favorite. Who would you choose?"

She's met a few of the hosts. In her role as Daniel's wife. At Oscar celebrations. Before she got tired of going to them.

A purple rubber band snaps across his fingers while he waits for her response. He is unable to be still. Linda's refusal to hear his apologetic confession, her refusal even to hear that the affair with Rosie is over, makes him edgy. His need to explain, to justify, to beg resolution leaks out in small repetitive body movements, tics. The rubber band breaks, snapping back against his hand.

"Do you think it's a good idea for an article?"

Fishing for approval.

Usually, she's the one who waits for approbation. The situation is reversed. Because as his audience she no longer reassures him with words. Because she observes and is not invested.

He can no long bear to wait for an answer.

"When did the doctor say you'd be able to talk?"

# 34. Open wide

"Very nicely healed."

Dr. de Boer looks pleased with himself. His work is done. Now it's up to Linda.

"Go down the hall, make an appointment with the speech therapist."

## 35. VOICE ISSUES, a case history.

Faith Raven may never finish the article, so disturbed was she by her conversation with Daniel in the hospital cafeteria. She can't accept the fact that she didn't hear the pain in his voice until he was gone. She has a feel for pain, an instinct. How could her ego have been so lost in fantasies about getting the article published that she didn't pay attention to the reality across the table from her?

She is tempted to call him and ask how he's doing. She could call with the pretext that she's asking about Linda. A legitimate reason. And then she could slip in the personal questions, express her concern. No, she can't do that. Linda, her patient, deserves her loyalty.

## 36. Ghost lover

The desert stranger visits Linda in her dreams.
Some nights he's so real she tastes the campfire in his
hair and stir-fry on his tongue.
Other nights, he's a radiance, a penetration of light.
Daniel sleeps, oblivious to these nocturnal visitations.
Linda wakes, luminous.
Is her infidelity greater than Daniel's?

# 37. Speech

A voice clinic. Linda is in a room with others — the nodules, the acute laryngitises, the laryngectomies. All ages, genders, sizes, colors. On a folding table, lined up in a row, an assortment of speech aids: the electro-larynx, the amplifiers, an array of batteries and filters, as well as nicely printed guides to electro-laryngeal and esophageal speech.

The room is quiet; no one is speaking because no one can, Linda belatedly notices. She takes a seat on a small schoolroom chair. The man next to her — in his fifties, with wavy gray hair and a polite David Niven mustache — whips out his notepad and scribbles quickly.

"You have lovely eyes."

She looks into his — gray, sad, trying to smile at her.

"Throat cancer," he writes. "What about you?"

She shakes her head. Her victory over a non-malignant cystic tumor seems paltry.

The speech therapist, Ms. Kitsle, a thin nervous woman, stands in front of them. She introduces a laryngectomee by name, Victor Avila, but to Linda he remains The Laryngectomee.

The electro-larynx, explains The Laryngectomee by means of a visual aid he holds up for everyone to read, is a handheld device about the size of a small electric shaver that has a vibrating plastic diaphragm.

It sounds sexual. Linda pictures what the desert stranger would do with such a device. Instinctively, her fingers touch her throat. The man next to her casts a sympathetic glance. Victor Avila then demonstrates speech by placing the end of the electro-larynx against his neck. A small button is pushed that causes the plastic diaphragm to vibrate, which produces a vibration in the throat that imitates the vibration of the vocal cords. Imitates. Not reproduces.

"As you can see, I am speaking." He smiles broadly.

"He sounds like Hal, the talking computer from 2001," the man writes to Linda. "Imagine him saying 'I love you' to his spouse." His sad eyes grow sadder. "I don't think it's for me."

It occurs to Linda she might be the only person in the room who has retained the potential of speaking normally. She feels guilty about the fact.

The Laryngectomee shows pictures of how air flow enters and exits the lungs through an opening in the neck called a stoma. Linda's new friend takes notes on esophageal speech in which sound is not produced by vocal folds (since there are none) but by vibrations in the esophagus. Air is swallowed and then allowed to escape in a controlled fashion, causing the walls of the esophagus to vibrate. This produces a sound, which can be articulated by the mouth and lips to produce speech.

It all sounds to Linda like so much trouble. Is speech worth it? Is it necessary to have a voice?

## 38. Scaling to high-C

After the clinic, she goes to the speech therapist's office. It is small, room only for one patient at a time. On the desk is a sculpture of a generic mouth and throat, cut in half so the inner workings of speech are visible. Positioned next to the mouth and throat, are life-like reproductions of true vocal cords both open and closed, as well as false vocal cords. Linda is surprised that false vocal cords exist.

Before she can reflect on their meaning...

Doe-Re-Me-La-Fo-Fa-Te-Doe.

Again and again. Perfectly pitched each time.

Ms. Kitsle, not Rosie.

A demonstration. The mountain which Linda will scale in the next few weeks. Ms. Kitsle's job is to help her relearn the basics. This time around, Linda will breathe and speak correctly. Like learning to sing, informs Ms. Kitsle, the rudiments of speech rehabilitation will be found in matching her tones to the scale.

"It's a matter of practice," she says.

Today is the first step. After a month of soundlessness, Linda must reproduce middle-C.

Ms. Kitsle positions her thumb and index finger so she can locate the vibration in Linda's vocal cord.

"After me," says Ms. Kitsle. "Doe."

Linda's throat muscles tighten. She can't imagine what she'll sound like, or how it will feel, actual vibrations bouncing off a newly-configured cord. What if nothing happens? What if Dr. de Boer inadvertently severed her larynx? What if Ms. Kitsle turns out to be another Rosie?

She inhales, waits. Her lungs deflate. She's not prepared. Unable to conceive what advantage words will give her, she puts her head between her hands and slips back into the great maw of silence that swallowed her in Death Valley.

"Let's try it now," urges Ms. Kitsle, her tuft of bangs fluttering anxiously, her chirpy tone threatening to lose patience.

Linda ignores her. She conjures herself in the Andes playing the Peruvian flute, the dangling feather dancing to her melody.

"Most people can't wait to get started."

I'm not most people, thinks Linda, but she straightens up. She doesn't want to disappoint Sam. He's planning on bringing her to school for show-and-tell.

She takes a deep breath and lets it loose. "Doe!"

A harsh scratch of a noise, acres away from middle-C, alarms Linda. She sounds like an injured animal in the African Savannah.

Again.

Doe.

Again.

Doe.

Again.

"Very good." Ms. Kitsle repeats the notes of the scale, emphasizing sounds, cocking her head to make sure Linda has heard. There's precision, but no music in Ms. Kitsle's repetition. She's a parakeet, not a canary.

"You may begin to speak at home, but articulate only one syllable at a time, and don't overdo it." She hands Linda a flash drive for her iPhone. "This has the scale. You only are to practice 'Doe,' nothing else, and bring the note to our next session."

In the car, Linda plays the note.

Ms. Kitsle's crisp voice: "Doe."

Linda repeats Doe. Wilted, flat.

Again. And again.

"Doe." The sound is slightly braver, almost resonating, but she is exhausted.

She drives past the pet store, slowing to see more clearly. Had they ever recovered the stolen canary? She wonders. She looks up in the trees, hoping for a glimpse of yellow feathers.

The voice of Ms. Kitsle persists. "Doe."

Linda forces herself to concentrate. "Doe," she tries.

Again.

"Doe."

Somewhere on Los Feliz Boulevard, between Hillhurst and Vermont, Linda matches her 'Doe' with Ms. Kitsle's. A true tone. Linda's fist shoots up in victory. She projects a 'Doe' so loud and clear and joyous that the man in the other lane with his window down hears her and smiles.

"Doe, a deer, a female deer...." The man will sing all the way into West Hollywood. "Ray, a drop of golden sun..."

Pizza parlor. Thin crust. Everything on it.

Him: "Girls always say they're not hungry, then they go home and raid the refrigerator."

Her: "Not me."

Watching her slide a section, dripping with cheese, into her mouth...

Him: "I am in complete awe."

"Of me eating pizza? I didn't think you were that easy to impress."

"What did you think?"

"Discerning. Great hair. High standards... probably impossible for mere mortals to meet."

"It's hard to meet standards. Meeting people is easier."

They smile at each other, the young Linda and Daniel, about to become a couple.

Conversations with Daniel.

Staying up all night discussing movies, old TV programs, new novels, the absence of irony in their college professors. Sharing ambitions.

Her: "I want to work with homeless teenagers and help them write."

Him: "I don't care what I do, so long as I'm famous. (pause) That's a joke." Comparing summer camp triumphs and high school traumas, offering each other aid and solace and the implicit promise that never will they turn into their parents.

Admitting weaknesses. "I haven't told this to anyone before, but..." It didn't matter what. Picking toe-jam, hating Thanksgiving, cursing slow drivers, being intimidated by horses, by Scandinavian super-models, by neurosurgeons

— ("Honestly, they know exactly which of my brain cells I murdered with tequila!") — every late-night confession bringing them closer.

She's comfortable with him. And he, with her. They fit.

Never bored, they could talk forever.

"What would you do with a million dollars?" He asks.

"I'd...oh my god, I don't know. I never thought about it," she responds.

"Sure, you did."

"No, honestly. From the time I was little, I trained myself not to dream about what I couldn't have."

"Then I'll have to."

"What?"

"Teach you how to dream."

\*\*\*\*\*

Linda slips into the house without being noticed. She wants to surprise her family. Daniel stayed home to be with Sam instead of getting a babysitter or arranging a playdate while she went to the voice clinic and speech therapist. He volunteered, which makes her wonder. He has switched from purple rubber bands to yellow ones, still snapping them on skin raw and punished. There have been no more calls from Rosie. No hems and haws from Daniel. No excuses.

She pauses in the entryway, and sings out, loud and clear, "Doe!"

Buried in the back office where he juggles a variety of applications to predict the audience share for the upcoming Oscars, Daniel is startled by the sonorous tone coming from the living room. He dreads that it is Rosie. Leaping from his chair, he runs the entire length of the house, determined to stop her before she hits the rest of the scale, before Sam asks why the singing teacher is there, before she jeopardizes his family, before his life turns into Fatal Attraction.

But it's not Rosie. It's his very own wife, hands on hips, head tossed back, glorying in middle-C. Relieved, he applauds.

"Mom's talking!"

His new-found enthusiasm skates off Sam, who doesn't glance up from his Lego, strewn all over the floor.

"'Doe' isn't talking."

"It's the first step," says Daniel. "Pretty soon she'll be saying something else, won't you?" He asks Linda. "Pretty soon we'll be having conversations!"

And life will be returned to normal.

"So, can you say something?"

Like what? wonders Linda.

Daniel waits. Conflicted, she takes her time, putting away her purse. Once she speaks, she'll have to continue speaking.

What sentence will make it worth giving up silence?

"Come over here, Sam," orders Daniel. "Let's listen to Mommy."

Sam sidles over to his Dad and joins him in waiting.

Linda shakes her head. She feels too self-conscious. She knows from the session with Ms. Kitsle that her voice sounds like John Hurt in The Elephant Man, a movie she and Daniel watched one night after Sam was asleep.

Sam gets restless. "See, I told you 'doe' wasn't talking!"

Daniel looks disappointed.

Linda touches his shoulder. She'll do it.

She steals a line from the movie.

"I-AM-A-HU-MAN-BE-ING!"

The utterance bursts forth, one gravelly syllable at a time, as though hewed in the belly of a giant. Such deep, unnatural intonation issuing from his wife disconcerts Daniel. Not that he was expecting breathy, sultry, dulcet — too much to ask for after the operation — but a freakish monotone, the kind of voice exhibited in sideshows of circuses, the kind that has to insist it's human because otherwise nobody would know —

Sam shrieks in mortal pain, "Tell her not to talk like that!"

He won't look at her. That is not her voice. She is no longer his mother.

Daniel readily complies. "Do you have to talk like that?"

Slow, measured Elephant Man speech. "YES. I. DO."

"NO!" Sam covers his ears and runs out of the living room.

Linda holds her hands out in a helpless fashion. Would they rather her not speak at all?

Seeking to bypass more syllables Daniel requests that she sing 'doe' again. He goes to the piano, and hits middle-C.

She responds, another 'doe' flowing out of her mouth.

He studies her, as if her face has been altered, a nose out of place, an eye askew.

"You're on key, you know that?"

And so she is.

Daniel has the piano tuned.

Linda masters the scale.

Ms. Kitsle is proud of her.

Sam no longer punishes his mother by running out of the room. He likes to sit under the piano while his parents sing. He puts his head against the wood and feels the reverberation.

The scale as music.

The scale as balance.

Daniel, who studied music through high school, adds half-notes and trills, arpeggios. He harmonizes.

Linda concentrates on each note, full and round. Sometimes she goes off.

Her ear is still in training.

Daniel repeats the phrase on the piano. He is patient as she tries to match the sound.

She aims for resonance. An opera singer is able to produce resonance at 2,500 Hz, which allows the voice to be heard above an entire orchestra. Linda strives to be heard as far as the other room.

The singing of scales becomes a nightly routine, not as satisfactory as tennis, but a start, as far as Daniel is concerned. Should Linda forget, after dinner, after dealing with dishes, with Sam, with unfinished items on her to-do list, he reminds her.

"Honey, let's rock and roll."

Linda is touched. In the evenings, he forgoes business dinners to stay at home and practice with her. The odd phone calls have stopped. She is sure that the affair with Rosie is over and is relieved there hadn't been an explosive confrontation, the kind where things are said — in her case written — that never can be unsaid. Whenever the whiff of suspicion creeps into her consciousness, she shoves it away. The stranger no longer visits her dreams.

Daniel runs his fingers up and down the keyboard, and she follows. Like a dance, she thinks. A dance with our voices.

Duet. Two as one.

Together they explore their way out of the labyrinth of marital dissonance.

For centuries, from Pythagoras of ancient Greece through the Renaissance, philosophers and composers, priests and poets, believed that music reflected the order and harmony that surely existed in the universe. The music of the spheres.

Maybe this was all worth it.

On the other hand ...

Tonality was detonated in the twentieth century. Clashing sounds, random choices, disjunction — pillars of a new fractured metaphysics of music. Under harmony, discord.

Inside Daniel's head: It's been over three weeks since I spoke to Rosie. Maybe she's gotten the message. She must have gotten the message. She's not dense. She got the message.

Inside Linda's: C-D-E-F-G-A-B-C.

And yet ...

Harmony is not negated. We respond to it. We find it beautiful. Surely, we are capable of acknowledging the random chaos of the twenty-first century while simultaneously cherishing a music in which two voices become one, scaling sequences all the way to heavenly spheres.

Linda gives herself over to the notes. They ring inside, vibrating through her entire body. The sensation is remarkable.

# 41. The message

If Daniel thought Rosie got the message, he was wrong. She phones him at work.

Unfortunately, Daniel's assistant is up to his neck in algorithms designed to rate the results of readers' votes for the best Oscar host of all time. He does not answer the phone.

Daniel picks up.

Rosie.

An edge, an attitude, blame. Selling magazine subscriptions? Really? How could he?

Does he fight against his impulse to apologize? If you'd asked him right before she called, he would have said with conviction, "It's over. She got the message."

His brain freezes. He apologizes. She murmurs that he's forgiven, and confesses that she's missed him, really missed him. He collapses, her soft murmur piercing his loins and all he wants is the feel of her in his arms and once more, he's willing to promise anything.

"Then take me to the Oscars," pounces Rosie.

It so happens two invitations sit on his desk the way they do every year, invitations to the Academy Awards. Linda never goes; she never wants to.

"Introduce me to important people," continues Rosie. "Allow me to shine and have people wonder who I am." She is describing a fantasy that has nurtured her since she was ten. No earlier. Since she was in kindergarten and belted out lyrics to The Orphan Girl ("I am an orphan on God's highway…") when asked to sing something, and she made the entire class cry.

Daniel can't do that. Even though Linda never goes, she

always watches with her friend, Stephanie, especially the beginning, the extravagant over-the-top display of fashion as stars strut their stuff on the Academy Red carpet — Academy Red, the real name of that particular color. Linda recognizes every actress, every designer, each piece of jewelry. He teases her about it, since she professes not to care about those things. She'd see him out there with Rosie. Even if Rosie were wearing a wig, she would know.

There's another reason, a better reason. The duets. He and Linda have been playing duets, the balance and harmony of scales bringing him closer to his wife than he's felt in a while, since she started therapy, in fact.

Rosie is off the scale. She's an aria of passion, but she's self-absorbed, wants only one thing from him, and it's not his penis, he knows that, try as he might to delude himself. It's a career she is after, him being Barry Gordy to her Diana Ross, Tommy Mottola to her Mariah Carey, René Angélil to her Celine Dion. There is no future for him with Rosie.

He will promise anything but Oscar night, he tells her.

"That is not okay with me," she responds.

# 42. Set point

Boxes are piled high in the garage, like a fort. Linda has vanished behind them. She's not hiding. She is sifting. Culling. In speaking one syllable at a time, she recognizes that too much verbiage can be a burden. The same is true about memories, she has decided, especially ones stored in cartons that never are opened.

Sam is sure his mom is playing hide and seek, and he searches for her in his favorite spot, a half-finished tree-house accessible only by a rope. Daniel, looking for her as well, passes the garage and notices stacks of boxes half-opened and in disarray. He should have known. His wife is there, shredded newspaper in her hair, holding a dead yellow rose coffined in a plastic bag.

"Sam and I have been hunting all over the place for you, Linda!"

She mentally deletes 'all over the place' as unnecessary verbiage. 'Linda' also, since no one else is in the garage.

"I am here."

She indicates the stuff she's been sorting. All kinds of stuff. Letters from grandparents, written on real paper with ink. Photo albums from Daniel's mother. Books from college. Wedding presents they hadn't liked but couldn't return; bargains bought wholesale by relatives, or because they'd fallen off the back of a truck, Daniel joked at the time.

"What's that?" He points to the bag in her hand.

Then he remembers. It is the boutonniere he wore when they were married. Linda's bouquet is long gone, having flown into the wildly waving hands of Stephanie who'd been her bridesmaid.

"Come on, Sam and I want to teach you tennis."

Linda sighs. She's been dumping memories all morning long. The trash is full of them. In the past she felt they'd disappear if objects weren't around to anchor them, but that's not true for her anymore.

She'd asked Daniel to help her, but he laughed and said, "Just get rid of it all."

The yellow rose disintegrates inside the plastic bag. She tosses it. Time for the making of new memories.

She stands up, takes Daniel's hand, determined to be a good sport.

"Let's play ten-nis." One syllable at a time.

She tries. She really does. For the sake of both Daniel and Sam. Every time she swings, they watch her with hopeful, expectant faces. Sometimes the ball connects and soars high over the net into the adjacent court. Sam happily runs to fetch it. Daniel murmurs encouraging comments like "great connect."

The more she tries, the more upset she becomes. It's not because she's bad at it. Linda isn't someone whose ego is invested in her athletic ability. But, alone on her side of the net, positioned between fault lines, she feels exposed, vulnerable. In her hand, the racket flaps and flails like a spastic glottis between her vocal cords, misdirecting every attempt to make contact. She starts to cry.

Daniel hurries towards her.

"What's wrong? It's only a game."

She loses all semblance of control. Without intention, hardly conscious, coming from nowhere, broken syllables twist through the tears.

"I will nev-er play with you as well as that wo-man ten-nis part-ner who once grabbed your balls and stuck her tongue up your ass!"

Daniel jumps over the net.

He's amazed that Linda remembers—he scarcely does—and he's relieved that she's not crying about Rosie. He cradles her face in his hands, reassuring her.

"Honey, I haven't thought about her for ages, and you don't have to play any better than you can. I'll be the one grabbing your balls from whatever corner of the court you hit them."

This makes Linda smile.

That night they make love.

# 43. The Oscars

Why doesn't Linda want to go to the Academy Awards?

Beneath the hoopla, it's business. A lot of suits. Executives, agents, deal brokers. Unless they've been nominated, or their PR needs tweaking, or they are beholden to the Academy, even the stars prefer private parties at chic restaurants where the show looks better on a television screen and you can eat during the speeches. Having gone once, then twice, she vowed never to go again, so bored was she by industry chitchat, and a burden to Daniel who was there as part of his job, who could chitchat more easily if she weren't at his side. Daniel is not interested in who wins or what's being worn; his focus is on the size of the broadcast audience, whether this year's share is larger than the one before, and if not, what does it mean. That's why she has a standing date year after year to watch with Stephanie.

Sunday morning of the big day, Daniel heads to his office early. From there he'll go straight to the Dolby Theater in the heart of Hollywood. Linda watches as he puts on a black Tom Ford suit and tie. Long ago he stopped wearing a tuxedo. "I hate cummerbunds, and nobody will notice," he'd said. "They're all way too preoccupied with their own appearance."

The truth is, he looks so handsome in his fitted suit, she contemplates the inconceivable — maybe she should go this time, because, maybe, this time it would be fun. She and Daniel haven't been out together since the night they went to the Ground Bean.

"You'll be at Stephanie's, right?" He asks.

She shrugs.

"I'll be back as soon as I can."

His kiss good-bye is unburdened by any feelings of guilt. He hasn't heard from Rosie. She may be brooding, but at least she isn't calling him.

His step wouldn't be so light or his relief so palpable if he'd witnessed her activities this past week: At the hairdressers, deliberating between cornrows with extensions, or an Ida Lupino up-style. At designer resale shops, trying on gowns, imagining whose famous skin had come in contact with the silk, the chiffon, the beaded glitter. At her favorite shoe store, blowing another month's salary on strappy sandals that melt like butter when touched.

Rosie hasn't been calling Daniel because it hasn't been necessary. She is in possession of one of his Academy Awards invitations.

The day after their unacceptable telephone conversation, she visualized a solution to her problem. A redressing of balance. She parked herself, discreetly hidden, across from his retro-neo-20th century modern office building until she saw Daniel depart for his lunch meeting, undoubtedly with a major honcho who could have gotten her a meeting with someone in the music division of any agency if only — here she stopped her mute tirade — and she sashayed into his office. Her waitress uniform, the top button undone, cleavage peeking with curiosity at the intern manning the front desk, was the perfect disguise.

"Daniel, that is, Mr. Gregory, left an Oscar invitation as a tip," she whispered conspiratorially. "But he forgot to actually give it to me."

The intern hesitated. Neither Daniel nor his assistant was there to confirm.

"Like in that movie," she quickly added. "Where whatshis-name gives half a lottery ticket as the tip, only his greedy wife gets hold of it and refuses to split it."

"Nicholas Cage. It Could Happen to You." He shot it out like he was on a game show.

Rosie was impressed.

"But Daniel's wife isn't like that," added the intern. "She's not greedy."

"Exactly," agreed Rosie. "Which is why, after an especially delicious lunch topped off by a slice of banana cream pie, his favorite, Mr. Gregory can give the invitation away, should he choose."

The intern, a product of a midwestern film department and brand-new to Hollywood and unaware of Academy rules, particularly the one dictating that invitations are not interchangeable, was swayed by Rosie's logic. However, since Daniel had not left any instructions, he put on his blank face and a polite smile and hoped the phone would ring so he could have an excuse not to look at her.

"Check to see if the invitation is here," she murmured, touching his little finger with her crimson nail. Her eyes were soft and limpid, like the heroine of a Harlequin romance.

That made sense to him. He found the envelopes casually placed in the side top drawer, along with a dry cleaners receipt and a box of Zantac. Two invitations. He took out the one with Linda Gregory's name, examining it for instructions or other clues. None were there. A quandary. If he gave it to this enchanting waitress, or if he didn't — either way he could lose his non-paying but resume-significant job. Film school hadn't prepared him for this.

"I'll leave my phone number with you." Her voice was intimate, a promise. "If there's a problem."

He hesitated. "It doesn't have your name on it."

"That's not a problem."

She removed her simple Rosie business card and with one hand pressed it tenderly into his palm, a distraction while her other hand slipped his iPhone under a slew of papers.

"Call Daniel," she said. "He'll vouch for me."

The intern nodded. A good idea. Until he began looking for his phone, and thus failed to see her hide the invitation into her uniform's front pocket.

"I have to get back to my shift," she said. "I'll thank you properly one day." She blew him a kiss.

The intern blushed.

He meant to tell Daniel, but by the time his boss returned, there were deadlines and fact-checking and a crisis due to a major agency threatening a boycott because an important actor-client vying for an academy award had been given short-shrift in one of their pre-Oscar columns. The fact of Rosie's unusual tip was lost in the swirl of office chaos.

Watching Daniel leave the house, Linda waffles on whether or not she should stop his car before it's out of the driveway, and confess how, inspired by their duets (more and more accomplished, garnering compliments from neighbors), she's conscious of the pleasure she receives in his company, a charge tinged with creative and sexual energy. When their separate notes hit the right register, intertwine, blend, transform into an entirely other sound, it becomes, for her, a metaphor for marriage. Should she tell him that she has decided she wants to go to the Oscars?

The impulse is there, surprisingly strong, but Sam yells from the kitchen that his oatmeal is too milky and he's not going to eat it. By the time she's spooned out some of the milk, added extra raisins, a sprinkle more of brown sugar, and a banana, and satisfied Sam's notion of what oatmeal is supposed to taste like, Daniel is long gone.

She drives over to Stephanie's, early in the afternoon. This way they can soak up the pre-pre-Oscar gossip. While slouched on the sofa next to Stephanie, flipping channels, taking in the fans who wait under the unflinching LA sky for a glimpse of their fave celebs, Linda is gripped by the overly-produced candid clips of young, beautiful actresses and the offerings of designer dresses they wear. It's not because these tempting creatures will be circulating around Daniel, who sees them all the time, and therefore is inured to them. What occurs to her, in such force that her Long Island tea spills all over Stephanie's latest needlepoint is this:

Last year she watched equally over-produced clips of a different group of actresses clad in a different set of gowns, gowns now consigned to resale along with more than a few of the young beautiful actresses who wore them. Last year's hot producers and directors aren't even on the radar. Storybook couples from a year ago are no longer holding each other's hand. In a SoCal climate without obvious seasons, the Oscars are a clarion call to remind us that time passes, and partnerships are not forever.

No more drifting. Linda intends to embrace her marriage with a whole heart. Otherwise, what's the point?

"I am go-ing down there!"

"And leave me here alone?" Stephanie wails.

"I owe it to him."

"Why? He's the one cheating!"

"That's o-ver. We've been sing-ing du-ets."

"Duets?" It's all Stephanie can do, not to roll her eyes.

Linda shrugs. "Yes, du-ets. Like you do-ing sal-sa with a part-ner. On-ly he is my hus-band."

She calls Daniel at his office. He's gone already. Even better. He always leaves her invitation at the VIP desk. This way she can surprise him.

"Come on," she says to Stephanie, "let me try on one of our sal-sa out-fits."

"As if."

Linda loves her friend's walk-in closet — an entire upstairs converted into a personal department store reflecting Stephanie's encyclopedic interest in style, ranging from antique southern belle ball gowns to futuristic wearable sculpture, mostly of Japanese design. When they were teens, Linda would go to Stephanie's house and they'd pull out eclectic styles from the indulged wardrobe and dress up as Harajuku girls, or goth vampires, the genre of the day always chosen by Stephanie, presumably because they were her clothes, but Linda never objected. To choose meant she'd have to exclude all the other choices which struck her as sad. Or fraught. Or arbitrary. Or scary. Or, and this she never admitted, wrong. Wrong because the choice would have been hers. Hers alone.

Inside her closet, Stephanie's mood brightens. She pulls out vintage Gaultiers and priceless Chanels and drapes them over Linda.

"Yes! Wow. Look!"

The gowns are beautiful on her. Transforming. Wasn't that what she thought to do when she briefly fantasized about dying her hair the color of Rosie's, sashaying up to her husband in a tight green skirt and 1940's slingback heels, saying, 'What do you think of me now?'

"As glamorous as the movie stars," pronounces Stephanie, "And I can do your makeup to match."

But Linda, being a Linda, and not a ZsaZsa or an Ava, or one of the new iconic names walking across the red carpet, changes her mind. She claims her ordinariness. She resolves to wear the same simple, elegant, tight black dress she had on the night she and Daniel went to NoHo to hear Rosie sing.

"But this Galliano is perfect for you!" protests her friend.

Linda is adamant. She plans to return to that moment in the coffee house and rewrite it.

Can she do that? Can she look at this whole novel as scrawl in the Ladies' Room, and with some super-powerful graffiti cleanser, wipe the wall clean?

If she could, what would it accomplish?

Let's postulate that Linda came out of the Ground Bean Ladies' Room before Daniel and Rosie locked eyes. That she introduced them directly, so it didn't enter Rosie's mind Daniel could help her career. And Daniel, instead of swooning into Rosie's song, was proud of his wife for choosing such an excellent voice instructor. Then what? The problem of narrative would still exist. Linda would still have to find her voice. She'd still have to find the courage to be wrong. There's the crux. Not whether or not her marriage with Daniel can survive Rosie.

Sam is excited. His mother is allowing him to stay up with the babysitter and watch the awards. He will look for her, he says, right next to his dad. The camera will be sure to show them because his dad is so important. "Right, Mom?" His eyes shine with pride. "Without Daddy," he says, "people wouldn't know what's what."

She says, yes, his father is important. "He's im-por-tant to us," she says, slowly, carefully, as she slips on the black dress, and she means it. Linda still speaks in single syllables, although Ms. Kitsle has told her to go ahead with phrases. The prospect makes Linda shy. More than one sound at a time seems too opulent.

She has Sam fasten the clasp of a pearl necklace. "We are fam-i-ly," she pronounces, tickled when Sam catches the reference and starts singing the tune. He sounds just like Daniel, in a higher register. They harmonize while she stuffs a purse with keys and money and her wallet. She kisses him on the forehead, leaving a lipstick print. He giggles.

The taxi honks.

She steps into the red stiletto heels and walks out.

"We are faamilleee," reprises Sam.

## 44. Spotlight

As soon as Linda's taxi merges onto the Hollywood Freeway, it is stuck in a traffic jam. Like shredded orange peel in chunky marmalade. Oscar jam. Happens every year. And, just like the rain, nobody's prepared. Commentators poke fun — movie stars caught in traffic, yuk, yuk. Stars are royalty, but on the freeway, egalitarianism rules.

A mile ahead, Rosie is stuck as well, Rosie in a sapphire blue gown that picks up the glow of her copper hair, Rosie embarking on a perfect evening, although not in the limo of her fantasy, not even an Uber or Lyft — none available even if she could afford it— but in her old Corolla with the stick shift, bald tires, and the patched paint job in need of a wash. A car that runs as much on hope as gas and duct tape. There is a thin wedding band on her left ring finger, bought at a Ninety-nine Cent store.

Daniel arrived early at the Hollywood and Highland Center. He already has braved the bleachers packed with eager fans, climbed the red-carpeted Grand Staircase leading to the Dolby Theater, and now he presses flesh, acknowledging new stars and old. He teases nominees, compliments the presenters, mingles with celebrities — on a first name basis with all. He pays no attention to frazzled tales of freeway congestion. He's not expecting anyone who might be delayed.

Static crackles. The dispatcher contacting Linda's taxi driver wants to know how long he'll be. "Gif or take a week," the cabbie says, glancing in the rearview mirror to see how his fare reacts to his wit.

Her smile is unrelated to his witticism. She is picturing how pleased Daniel will be, the goofy grin he sometimes gets when he's really happy. It's been too long since she's expressed interest in what he's doing, and what better way than showing up for the Awards? Maybe it's the Rosie effect, but so what? she almost asks the driver. If Rosie's infatuation with Daniel has caused Linda to appreciate him more, if it's pushed her out of a rut and into the Oscars, live and in person, her head next to his, viewing the show with him instead of Stephanie, isn't that all for the better?

Sam's joyous refrain, "We are faam-i-ly" echoes.

The cabbie might have cautioned against it. Coming from a part of Eastern Europe that saw violent shifts, betrayals, starvation and devastation, he might say, let well enough alone, and exit the nearest off-ramp and head back to Stephanie's on the opposing freeway lanes which, unlike the one they are on, are moving swiftly, without snarls or delays. She would not have listened.

A titanium Tesla, a hundred thousand dollar-plus Ludicrous Speed Model X revs hyper-fast and cuts Rosie off. She honks, loud and hard.

"My one big chance, and this asshole thinks he can cut in front? No way!"

She swerves into the next lane, accelerates, and seconds before rear-ending a monster semi, she slides back into her original lane, directly in front of the Tesla asshole. Now it's his turn to honk. She flips him off.

Rosie is in fine form, determined to arrive while the red carpet is vibrant, the fans enthusiastic. Once off the freeway, there are other hoops of fire through which she must jump. An excruciating descent into the Hollywood and Highland Center parking lot. The line snail-paced as special event parking passes are shown to security attendants. In spite of Rosie's dazzling smile, the attendant frowns. Suspicious of the junker she's driving, he looks underneath to see if explosives are attached. But after checking and rechecking the pass against her driver's license, he waves her on.

Thanks to Juan, a fry-cook at Joe's Diner, the license looks legitimate. She'd heard him discuss fake IDs for undocumented immigrants during his breaks — her Spanish is excellent, having studied Flamenco canciones — and she begged him to produce one for the Oscars. After she promised to share her tips for a month, plus go to his cousin's quinceanera so his Mama would stop nagging about finding a novia, he fabricated a California license in the name of Linda Gregory with Rosie's photo and stats. He did such a good job, that, except for the absence of embedded information, it could have fooled the DMV.

"Can't help you there," he admitted. "But if you're caught, you're still my date for the quinceanera."

Once through the parking garage, more security checks and body scanning. She opens her pearled clutch bag, shows the ID again and again, along with the invitation and her most winsome expression. She is ready to take on the world. Ready to shine. At the final inspection, an eagle-eyed guard looks up from the fake driver's license. He squints slightly. She shows no fear.

"You look beautiful today, Mrs. Gregory."

He personally escorts her into the hallowed portal. She melts in the throng milling under the dome in the enormous foyer. The glamor does not disappoint. She is Cinderella at the ball.

"And who might this picture of loveliness be? Where did you get that fabulous blue dress?"

One of the fashion commentators taps Rosie on the shoulder, making sure they are facing the cameras.

Before Rosie can say, the manager of Out of the Closet

saved it for me, it's a vintage Pierre Balmain, the commentator realizes her mistake. The commentator has a photographic memory for faces. Rosie is a nobody, not even a blip on the radar. She drops her hand and hustles over to the British actress who looks like a washed-out fairy princess in her cream tulle ballerina length dress, (Rosie's assessment), and coos enthusiastically about the brilliant performance those Brits always give.

Daniel is nowhere to be found, but Rosie doesn't care. Nothing can puncture the bubble she's floating in. She nonchalantly poses near celebrities; people nod as if they know her, then shake their heads, not sure. At the sight of music impresario Rick Rubin with his bushy gray beard presiding over a gaggle of Grammy award singers, her heart doesn't skip a beat. Au contraire. Exuding the conviction of someone who's been told her dress is fabulous, she bounces up as though he's been waiting for her all his life.

"Hi!" she begins. "I'm Rosie."

Like a laser, Daniel descends on her. "What are you doing here!"

She kisses him, effusively. "My Prince Charming! This is the best day of my life."

"We have to talk," says Daniel, his stomach twisting as he tries to pull her away.

"Thank you for this!" She waves the invitation under his nose, daring him to contradict her. "My first Academy Awards," she beams at Rubin, Daniel tugging, Daniel envisioning his wife and Stephanie watching. They never fail to watch, their sharp critical eyes assessing every démodé misstep.

"Danny-boy, don't be so eager," says Rubin. "What's the name again, sweetheart?"

"Rosie, Mr. Rubin. Just plain Rosie."

Linda is dropped off as near to the entrance as permitted. Two grim-faced sentinels, on the alert for impostors and terrorists, stop her. A scanner waves over her body. No alarms go off. She's directed to the VIP station, where her invitation waits, joining a queue of luminaries, huffy they haven't been recognized.

"You know who I am, don't you?" "Yes, Mr. Very Important Person, but I still have to verify your identity."

When it's her turn, giving each separate syllable equal weight as usual, she requests her invitation.

There is none waiting for her.

She refuses to believe that is true. Every year Daniel has left one for her, even though she's never gone. "In case you change your mind," he'd say. But he didn't say that, not this morning. Or did he? She can't remember. She begs the Academy Hostess to check all in-coming messages. None from Daniel. She texts him. Of course, he's not looking at his phone. Of course, he doesn't hear it in all the hoop-la. It may be hours before he checks for texts. She thanks the Academy Hostess, and looks around purposefully, as though her husband will appear.

Giving herself time to think, she goes to a Security Guard. She writes a request to please contact her husband, Daniel Gregory, of E-tainment, and tell him she's arrived, so please come and fetch her.

The Guard shakes his head. "No can do," and he blocks further entry.

Linda is upset that she didn't tell Daniel she wanted to come.

Does she give up?

Not when she's so close to surprising him with her unexpected presence. Not now.

Scenarios of sneaky and illegal ingress tap dance in her head. Diversion tactics. Forgotten marbles in her purse, confiscated from Sam when he wouldn't stop shooting in the kitchen, a collection of aggies and steel bollies. She lets them fall, and while attendees lose their balance, she dashes inside. Or she could hi-jack a TV camera, push through the crowd, frantic she'll be late to record the opening monologue. Too implausible.

Better to mill about, looking for someone she knows. A starlet with a back bare to her butt, for instance, who recognizes her as Daniel's wife and gushes about some wonderful article he wrote. They could hook arms and, posing for the cameras, walk together into the crush where they stand on the famous carpet, lightbulbs flashing in front of the white and gold Oscar banner, becoming part of the endless eye candy devoured by the public one piece after the next, never sated.

That particular starlet, unfortunately, is nowhere in sight.

Linda goes back to the VIP table. Her slow speech, in contrast to everyone else's hysteria, commands the attention of the Academy Hostess.

"I am mar-ried to Dan-iel Greg-ory. He publishes E-tain-ment Guide."

"You said."

"I need to speak to your Sup-er-vis-or." As the Hostess hesitates, "Now."

The Supervisor is brought over. She is a harried woman, her make-up starting to run under the pressure of bright lights and a torrent of last-minute snafus.

"Yes?" She scrutinizes Linda, as if wondering what kind of stunt this lady is trying to pull. "You may or may not be his wife," she says, "but we don't have your invitation, or any proof you were invited."

Linda takes out her wallet. She shows her driver's license. The Supervisor is not moved.

"I saw Mr. Gregory go in," the Academy Hostess admits. She finds Daniel's name on her tablet. "Here he is. He came alone."

Linda proceeds to pull out all the ID's that list her as Linda Gregory: AMEX, Visa, MasterCard, Bloomingdale's, Triple A, library cards. The Supervisor remains unimpressed. Linda wishes she had a Tiffany's or Barney's charge card, maybe they'd be more convincing. Finally, she finds a museum membership card made out to both their names: Linda and Daniel Gregory.

"See. I am not a ter-ror-ist. I am his wife."

Supported by her deliberate phrasing, she sounds very certain.

While they pour over the membership card, she debates whether to use the 'husband card,' something she has never done. If ever, now's the moment. She will not back down. She's the jaguar she once dreamt about, ready to pounce. She's the red-tailed hawk in the hills near her house, circling on currents of air higher and higher before it dives in for the kill.

Without Linda noticing, her syllables elide together when she speaks, the phrasing of a sentence back to normal. "My husband will be upset if you do not let me in." She pauses significantly. "I do not have to remind you that he is the one who decides what will be written in E-tainment." The implication being that the full force of the website will fall wrathfully on their shoulders, that, in editorial after editorial, the Motion Picture Academy will be castigated for denying her entrance.

"I did see him go in," reiterates the Hostess.

The Supervisor has already made out a pass.

In spite of the flotsam and jetsam on the Boulevard, in spite of (or maybe because of) the giant plaster statues based on the Babylon set from D.W. Griffith's Intolerance, the actual entrance to the Hollywood and Highland Center with its Grand Staircase bordered by art deco columns, Best Picture for each year in backlit fonts, and its enormous domed roof summons a certain solemnity. Linda pays no attention, hurrying up the stairs and into the much less impressive lobby of the Dolby Theater where there is neither glitz nor glamor, unless one counts the profusion of gold statuettes, and the gowns and jewels adorning women emerging from the bathroom, hurrying to the auditorium.

She follows bejeweled ladies into the theater. Circumventing camera platforms and dodging ushers, she navigates the aisles in the last mad moments before the show starts. She bumps into jittery nominees, famous directors, and powerful studio chiefs as she keeps looking.

"So sorry," she apologizes. "I seem to have lost my husband."

She has no idea where Daniel is sitting.

"It's a zoo in here. Maybe these will help." An older woman hands her a set of binoculars. "I always bring them. That way, when I'm bored, I check to see who's had a face- lift."

The chatter begins to subside. The stage remains dark, but the audience wants the show to begin.

Linda adjusts the focus and sweeps across the audience, noticing the emerald pendants and perspiration beads, Botoxed foreheads, bee-stung lips and pasted smiles. She recognizes actors. She sees people she's met at dinner parties. A mother from Sam's school who asked her to volunteer in the library. A father whose son is on Sam's soccer team. She is reminded how small the entertainment world is, even for her, a peripheral adjunct. So small it practically fits into one room, and yet, the entire globe is tuned in for this event.

More familiar faces, maybe because she's watched their movies or seen them in commercials. But no Daniel. A few disgruntled people around her are motioning for her to sit down. She ignores them and tilts the binoculars up towards the box seats on either side of the stage. First one side. And then, the other.

It doesn't take long.

## 44. The Academy Award goes to…

A steady pan. The high-powered lens zooms in on the rows of the box to the right of the stage, past three Versaces, two Pradas, one Miu Miu, as well as a plethora of new designers who are counting on the free loan of their gowns to garner them attention. Sapphire blue spills into and then floods the lens. Linda angles the binoculars ever so slightly. Rosie's face comes into frame. A minor shift; the torso and head of Daniel complete the picture.

They whisper to each other, exuding an intimacy that burns through Linda's entire being, or at the least her chest, pectoralis major and minor, unprotected smooth muscle tissue torched by pain, collapsing against her lungs, pressing out the air until breath is impossible. The sight of the two of them together, Rosie's copper hair brushing against Daniel's cheek, (the cheek Linda's fingers traced after their third date in an effort to memorize it forever) has a potency which prior abstract knowledge about their liaison failed to convey. The floor vanishes. She grabs onto the seat of the lady whose binoculars she borrowed, dizziness about to topple her.

The mother from Sam's school turns towards her in slow motion, a burgundy shawl sheltering her shoulders. The mother is a famous person, Linda's brain stops to remember. Famous because she's married to a more famous person, a man with his own talk show and a drinking problem who isn't in the empty seat next to her because he's probably at the Dolby bar getting soused.

"Sit down," someone whispers.

The father whose son is on Sam's soccer team also moves in slow motion and his smile of recognition fades as he sees that she is alone without a seat. He directs cop shows and has won an Emmy. He adores his wife, who is eight months pregnant, who sits next to him tapping his shoulder very slowly, so slowly it's imperceptible. Don't look at her, Linda can almost read the woman's lips, she's just been betrayed by her husband.

Everything slows down. Scientists have postulated that we could live longer than our designated life spans if our metabolism crept instead of walked, or walked instead of ran, and we could induce this with drugs, as they have with mice, or as some folks have done by fasting. But Linda is not interested in a longer life span. She does not use those seconds in which body shock freezes time to question whether the intimacy might be a visual illusion, a lie, created in part by the binoculars through which they are framed. She doesn't wonder if this is the moment that Daniel is telling Rosie he won't be seeing her anymore. She can't hear the words he actually says, to wit: "I'm married, and I want to stay that way." Linda sees only their closeness, a raw reality that rips away any veneer of accommodation on her part. Daniel is a stranger who belongs to someone else.

Did she predict this beforehand? Had murkier aspects of her unconscious come up with a scenario in which she knew, or might possibly have known, and really that's why she's here? Seeking a public arena in which to confront her husband? All of Hollywood, plus one billion viewers as far away as China eavesdropping on what she has to say? Or is that what we want — author and reader united in desire for climax, the big bang of catharsis?

The audience senses the Oscars is about to begin. A hush.

Linda inhales from deep inside the vortex, from the bottom of the bottomless pit. On her own, without supervi-

sion, she inhales a mighty combination of oxygen and prana. Her molecules had been rent asunder, and now they
reconfigure. She straightens up. The dizziness subsides.
She hands the binoculars back to the woman.

"Are you all right?" whispers the woman.

"Yes," Linda says, sure about it, finally. "I am."

She faces the box seats, perched over the side of the
stage. Music plays. Rainbow lights illuminate suspended
columns of thin crystal, strung together to create a tower in
the air. The moment has arrived.

Her voice soars out, a song, the syllables gliding
smoothly, projecting at 2,500 Hz. Ms. Kitsle would be very,
very proud.

"Daniel Gregory!"

Heads crane. Who is Daniel Gregory? Who is the beautiful albeit distraught woman in the simple black dress
standing alone in the aisle? Where are the Security Guards?

"I can see you!" The song continues.

There is a phenomenon known as resonance. When
human voice hits a high note that matches the natural frequency of crystal or glass, it displaces near-by air particles and they crash into the glass like invisible waves. If
the note is loud enough, it can cause the object to vibrate
so vigorously it shatters. In a 1970s commercial for Mem-
orex speakers, Ella Fitzgerald demonstrates this fact with
a wine glass.

Waves of sound strike the crystal columns. A sonic
wind.

Daniel rises in order to see who's calling out.

Her voice is so clear, so powerful, on key, rising higher
and higher, an aria. "It's over! I am no longer Linda Gregory. I am no longer Linda."

The crystal columns shiver and sway.

"Call me Simone!"

The audience relaxes, thinking this is part of the opening. It shouts in unison, "Call her Simone!"

Daniel sinks back into his seat.

"Call her Simone!"

Rosie, caught up in the moment, joins the chant.

With one long deep breath from the diaphragm, and perfectly pitched vibrations against her newly healed vocal cords reaching 3,000 Hz. or more, Linda projects, "I have a voice!"

The orchestra, ordered to counteract the disturbance, tunes up for a grand show biz overture. The piano, the string section, the horns, all hit High-C.

The scale soars from Linda's mouth, louder than the orchestra. "Doe! Ray! Me! Fa! So! La! Te!" Higher and higher, until it matches the first violin's High-C. "Doe!"

The columns vibrate violently. The crystal shatters. A Hollywood tower of Babel cascades down towards the audience, a torrent of glittering prisms of light.

Women scream, trying to protect their bare shoulders from falling shards. Men cover their heads with tuxedo jackets.

Linda closes her mouth.

The most common term used then and later on was 'meltdown.'

We could use it also. Linda had a meltdown. An easy explanation. Most of us either have had one or witnessed one. But it's the wrong word. It does not give her enough credit. Linda stood in the aisle of the Dolby Theater, surrounded by movers and shakers in Hollywood, by the shining lights of the industry, by the beloved idols of viewers all over the world, and she ignored them, looking past that high octane Oscar crowd, riveting her focus on Daniel and

Rosie. Instead of equivocating, instead of retreating into a series of narrative tweaks, or a convenient plot adjustment, instead of an edit, or delay-by-thesaurus tactic, she grabbed the proverbial dice and threw them, hard. The ivories could have bounced out of sight. They could have turned up snake eyes. But Linda, our Linda, took a chance. She risked her voice. By risking it, she found it.

## 45. Call me Simone

Inevitably comes the aftermath.

Remnants of shattered crystal hang like frozen rain-drops in the air. A Security Guard charges down the aisle, and trips on the over-sized swag bag placed in the aisle by a guest who'd retrieved it early— stuffed to the gills with give-away tokens worth thousands of dollars. Others follow, live action figures, lethal weapons drawn. FBI agents converge, awkwardly camouflaged by rented gowns and tuxedos. People in nearby seats hit the ground, imitating the movies that they have come this day to celebrate at the Awards ceremony. Linda holds her arms up in the air, less a gesture of submission than a blessing of the faithful. The guards don't shoot her. As for the FBI, primed for bomb threats or a 3D printed AK-47 in the hands of a high-tech Silicon Valley Ted Kaczynski, it hesitates to charge her with terrorism.

"She's a jealous wife," one agent observes. "Who can blame her, the husband showing up with another woman like that, at the Oscars."

Unable to pinpoint the cause of fractured crystal to anything other than her voice, and moved by her situation, they agree she should be under psychiatric supervision, suicide watch, plied with meds, tranquilizer infusions, and bed rest. She rejects those scenarios.

"I'm not the character in The Yellow Wallpaper," she tells them.

Their expressions are blank. They haven't read the short story. They don't know what it signifies. As far as they are concerned, she needs psychiatric supervision. Her next sentence proves their point.

"I'm not trapped in a child's nursery, scratching off wall-paper with my fingers," she says, "held against my will by my husband."

The agents look at each other, then glance up to the box seats, where said husband, utterly humiliated by this public denouncement, makes his way towards the exit assisted by a stunned usher. The other woman doesn't move, reluctant to leave her first red carpet event before it starts. The usher returns for her. Without further discussion, of one mind, the Feds escort Linda aka Simone out of the theater while a crew sweeps up the shards, and the glib, quick-witted comic host in charge of keeping the show running on time cracks a few ad-libbed jokes so everyone can settle back into the more agreeable suspense of who wins what.

Once outside, Linda, now emphatically Simone, looks around. Paparazzi rush to photograph her. Fans crane their necks to see what the commotion is about. Hollywood Boulevard turned into a command post for the hypothetical attack on the Dolby Theater. Cop cars flash red, amber and blue. Officers patrol the street, guns pulled. A SWAT team is on route. The FBI's grip on her arms tighten. It occurs to Simone that this is a serious big deal.

She drops mention of The Yellow Wallpaper. She has nothing to gain by edifying government agents about the author, Charlotte Perkins Gilman. In fact, she's surprised it came up, never one of her favorite stories — too fervid for her taste. Striking a reasonable tone, she looks her captors straight in the face and insists that she is quite sane, that her voice with its shocking effect surprised her as much as it surprised the rest of the world, and, most persuasive, a good citizen, she says firmly, "I take full responsibility for the damage I inadvertently caused."

The Feds turn her over to the police.

She spends the night in jail.

A description here is unnecessary. Whatever the jail-house scene, it's been covered so many times and in so many ways, we know all the variations. Garish prostitutes, leering lesbians, vicious women of different colors, in gangs, or destitute, homeless and/or drug addicted, enraged, deluded, possibly rabid fanatics of political, religious, sectarian 'isms', hyped-up martyrs of conscience, all somehow coming together to threaten the nice middle class lady who really has no business being in prison — we can skip it altogether. Especially since it has no bearing on Simone's experience.

The police would have released her to Daniel, but he is nowhere to be found, ditching Rosie, hiding his face from the photographers behind the bag of swag, rushing straight home, where the babysitter gives him a funny look and before he can say anything, before he can explain, justify, excuse himself, the sitter rushes out the door. Sam cries because his dad shouts at him when he says he saw Mom on TV and asks why her new name is Simone, and where is she, and why didn't she come back with him, and Daniel struggles for answers, his anger with Linda for what she's done conflicting with his concern that she might be dangerously unstable.

Stephanie retrieves Linda from jail the next morning, thus sparing her the indignities that would have occurred if she'd had to spend a second night. It should have been easy, since there was no bail, and her release merely a bureaucratic formality. But when Linda was booked, she signed in as Simone, no husband, no last name. The two cups of hand-crafted roasted coffee Stephanie brought are ice cold before she is able to prove to the correction officers and their supervisor that Linda and Simone are one and the same person.

Stephanie is mystified by her oldest and best friend who expresses zero gratitude. There are no apologies for the inconvenience. She acts like she deserved to be rescued, like she hadn't disrupted the entire Academy Awards, creating the equivalent of a major earthquake the damage was so bad, although, strangely enough, nobody was hurt, causing internet speculation for months afterwards, aliens being the most popular interpretation.

When asked to explain herself, all Simone says is, "No one should have to do jail time for a name change."

She's dropped off at home. Stephanie, piqued by the bad attitude and lack of a thank you, does not hang around. To Linda/Simone, the house feels foreign; the furniture off; Daniel, a stranger.

Sam runs to her, crying, "Mommy, Mommy."

She takes him to his room and plunks him down and explains that she has lots of stories to tell him about what happened, but right now she and his Daddy need to talk.

She approaches her husband.

No niceties. No asking of questions.

The marriage is over. No drama. Just the fact.

Daniel protests. "Don't say that, Linda, please. You're basing it on a gross misunderstanding. I did not invite Rosie to the Oscars. You have to give our marriage a chance."

"My name is Simone."

"You've got to believe me. The idiot intern let her take the invitation, but I had no idea. She was not my guest. It was over, and that's what I was telling her."

"You're repeating yourself."

"Linda, there has to be a way I can make this right. Please."

He would go on his knees but she turns her back on him. "My name is Simone."

She takes Sam with her to the neighborhood of Mount Washington, where she follows up on a listing of a bungalow she'd seen on Craig's List.

How is she able to move so quickly, we might ask? She had spent the night talking to her cell mate who told her about this particular bungalow. The woman had been the tenant until she was found guilty of embezzling the landlady.

Simone likes the bungalow.

She asks Sam if he likes it. "Yes," he says. "Why?"

She likes the landlady. She rents it.

Days later, she and Daniel convene in a lawyer's office.

After he reiterates for the tenth and last time that it wasn't his fault Rosie was there, she says, "That's not the point."

"Then what is the point, Linda? What is the goddamn point?"

"You won't deal with me as Simone. You don't even try. That's the point."

A look of such sadness and loss crosses her face that Daniel knows better than to argue. He also knows that Linda was the woman he loved. She was the familiar. She was the confidante for his hopes and dreams, his fears. She was his partner in building their family.

Simone is the unknown. Simone is disruptive. Simone scares him.

## 46. What happens now

Simone doesn't abandon the narrative, entirely.

She is still Sam's mother, although as Simone, she's a single mom who lives in a wooden bungalow with an overgrown garden that she rents from a middle-aged landlady, an optimist who trusts that this new tenant with a young son won't embezzle her.

The landlady owns a secondhand shop. She provides Simone with beaded scarves and antique fans silkscreened with portraits of reclining women.

When Simone hesitates, wondering why they're being offered, the landlady responds, "Don't overthink it."

Simone considers this good advice and vows to apply it to the rest of her life.

The furniture also comes from the second-hand shop. Simone refinishes each piece, proud of her work. Sam assists, carefully painting the kitchen table in the lime green he chooses with his mom, the chairs in apple red. It takes him a while to get used to the situation. He refuses to acknowledge her name, either the old one or the new one.

"I don't have to. Your name is Mom. That way I'm not confused."

This earns him a hug. "Clarity," Simone says. "That's what I'm aiming for."

She selects only the objects she intends to use. As Linda, she was equipped for a lifestyle she didn't lead – decanters for fine wines and matching goblets paired with each course of the dinner parties she never gave, Siberian down for the minus-zero degree weather that never happens in Los Angeles, caviar spoons, Irish linen guest towels, uneaten tins of smoked oysters and pates. Simone is able to look at a sterling silver soup ladle that her landlady waves in front of her, and say, no, I'll never use it. On the other hand, she doesn't turn down tools or invitations to dinner.

Men are drawn to Simone in a way that Linda never experienced.

"You're a guy magnet," observes the landlady, slightly jealous.

Simone shrugs. It comes with the name, what can she say? Plus, and this she does not realize, a hint of desert clings to her, the whisper of sage and palo verde, a scent lending mystery, long after the Linda-ness of her previous self has been shed.

Her new persona no longer reaches for Jungian archetypes or ancient myths to augment her existence. As much as we might have enjoyed those fabled excursions into the psyche with and without Dr. Raven's participation, and wish for them to continue, Simone is content with the day to day quality of her life. She finally did read The Iyengar Way, given to her by her landlady who has a yoga practice, and she appreciates the insight about breath. Her lungs can now inhale prana, the life force, without difficulty, without danger, and she accepts Mr. Iyengar's contention that this connects her to the cosmos in tasks as small as cleaning out bird cages. The truth is, she doesn't give it much thought.

She works full-time in the pet store. At first the other clerks are suspicious. They had known her as the polite customer who never bought anything but goldfish for her son, and who certainly didn't need to work in a neighborhood pet store. She wins them over with her tale of shattered crystal and a night in jail. It turns out she is very good with both animals and people. Since she has been there, puppies have stopped whimpering, the land tortoises smile, and chameleons cheerfully change from pink to blue and back again; sales have improved, complaints have dropped. After much discussion, and the printing out of research data, she convinced the owners to avoid puppy mills and to report illegally imported rare birds.

A retired podiatrist comes in every afternoon. Romance is not part of the picture. He misses talking to his patients, and Simone invites conversation with an ease that he associates with barkeeps. The pretext is buying food as well as small-scale exercise equipment for his grandchild's hamster.

"Since when can't dogs eat chicken bones?" he asks, referring to a prior argument. "What are we so afraid of?" He hands her a bag of hamster mix. "My father let Blackie, that was his bulldog, eat all the dinner scraps. You'd think Blackie would've choked to death, the fuss people make today. He never choked and food wasn't wasted. You could feed the entire homeless population on what gets thrown out today. My daughter doesn't let her son walk to school. She claims she'd get arrested for child neglect. A society of scaredy-cats if you ask me."

"Maybe we've become oversaturated with information," says Simone, ringing up the purchase. "We can't separate the facts that really matter from the ones that don't."

He nods, agreeing so vigorously, he almost forgets the hamster mix.

She gives it to him, adding, "But I still wouldn't give your dog any chicken bones."

Surrounded happily by allergens, after school Sam comes to play with the puppies and listen to the canaries sing.

He helps Simone clean out the fish tanks. Not a single goldfish dies. "Because I get rid of the poop," explains Sam.

The adjustment isn't as difficult as Simone expected, though once in a while she misses Linda.

She tries to explain to her landlady. "Linda was brave in a way that Simone doesn't have to be. What she did took courage, you know?"

Having never met Linda, the landlady doesn't know, nor is she curious about her. Simone lets it go.

She and Daniel come to an agreement. Simone doesn't want much, only her son, and for Daniel to take care of his health insurance, school fees and extras like summer camp. Daniel doesn't argue, except he wants guaranteed time with Sam. He puts a hefty sum of money into an account. It's in Simone's name, but he explains to her that it is in memory of Linda. The expression on his face is so forlorn, Simone feels like giving a comforting hug for his loss, but she doesn't. Instead, she agrees to let Sam live part-time with his dad.

We've already established that Daniel is a good father, and he should have his son part-time. For this transitional period, we'll allow him a tall lady-surfer from Australia, whose humor and alternative world view — i.e. waves are what matter — help ease his broken sense of life. She is kind to Sam, calls him Squid.

Rosie never sees Daniel again. She doesn't try, nor does she pursue the introduction to Rick Rubin. From a place deep inside her, one she rarely accesses, Rosie comprehends that never, no matter how much she practices, will she be able to hit that amazing high C which her first and only student, Linda, "call me Simone", had sung out in the Dolby Theater for the entire world to hear. And if perchance she did hit such a note, never would it be heard by a billion listeners.

Rosie takes a while to digest the event she witnessed at the Academy Awards, inextricably entwined with Daniel's dumping of her. Rehashing it over and over eventually becomes unproductive, like chewing on tasteless gristle. The time has come for her to do something. She waits for a new moon. At the top of Mulholland, avoiding Deadman's Curve aka Suicide Gulch, she casts a baleful eye over the valley, now a vast swath of disappointment where potential fans no longer boost her hopes. As the moon rises, Rosie lights the candle from the Laundromat and begins her incantation.

"Leave my mind. Leave my body. Leave my spirit so I can flourish."

With Saint Mary Magdalene as her witness, she exorcises Daniel Gregory and the entire Oscar episode from her life.

Does it work? Does a female Saint from the 1st century AD, who, according to miscellaneous religious texts and human anecdote, is imbued with compassionate understanding of the push and pull of sexual tides as well as the power of unconditional love, does this Saint also understand the compulsion to sing one's own song, to be heard by more than a small motley crowd at the Ground Bean? Do we imagine Mary Magdalene forgiving the sin of ambition that Rosie may or may not have committed? Does she — can she — intervene?

Judge for yourself.

One evening, Mr. Gus Santini and Miss Robin Luther return to Joe's Diner.

"It's my birthday," Mr. Santini says, "and we drove in from Palm Springs so I can celebrate with my favorite waitress."

Welcoming him with a vivacious smile, Rosie unbuttons the top button of her uniform, fluffs her hair, and then plants herself directly in front of Mr. Santini. She sings Happy Birthday full throttle. He and Miss Luther applaud, as does everyone else in the diner, with shouts of 'brava' and 'encore.' Thus encouraged, she sings a medley, including jazz songs and a rousing rendition of Puff, the Magic Dragon, Mr. Santini's favorite song from when he was a whole lot younger.

"I'm sixty-nine today," he tells Rosie. "And I want to give myself the gift of your voice. Tell me how. What should I do?"

Unlike the false promises clogging Rosie's past, this one happens. Even more unexpected, when you think about it, which she does, with gratitude, the guitar player at the Ground Bean is acquainted with someone who knows someone who gives the end product to another someone, and lo-and-behold, Rosie, her self-titled digital release, becomes a favorite on public radio. Rosie's career as an indie singer is born. Whether this is due to Mary Magdalene's intervention or not, the Saint's candle is enshrined in Rosie's bathroom next to a fancy box of matches. It is the light that guides her, especially during power outages.

Stephanie makes an effort. She phones Simone, careful to call her by the new name, and suggests lunch, dinner, salsa dancing, movies, shopping, massages at a Korean spa that advertises mineral baths, including one with healing mugwort, all women, and no clothing allowed.

Simone relents. "Ok. I'll meet you at the spa."

There she avoids the sulfur pool, with its faint stink of Margareta who howled at the moon, and she chooses the mugwort pool instead. When Stephanie joins her, she attempts to explain her distance.

"We no longer share a history. In Junior High, if I had been Simone, we wouldn't have been friends."

"Why not?" Stephanie tries not to be hurt.

A lady approaches the mugwort pool. She drops her towel and robe. Her body is bone thin, with a shaved pubis. Watching her descend, flesh submerged in water, Simone wonders if nakedness makes it easier to be honest. She puts it to the test.

"Because you always were the one who decided what we would do, and Linda always went along. If I'd been Simone back then, we would have fought about everything. Our wills would have collided. Not even Schopenhauer could have drawn us together."

Stephanie is bereft.

"You'll find another friend," says Simone.

"You are the person who knows me the best."

"This happens. People change and so do their friends."

"You think I won't understand how you've changed? Do you think you have surpassed me somehow? Honestly, are you any different from all those assholes who the minute they become rich and famous drop their BFs?"

"I need to figure out who Simone is."

"Fuck Simone."

"Like I said."

They look at each other. Simone sees that Stephanie's pain is deep-felt and genuine. Similar to Daniel's, it occurs to her. They both care about Linda in a way that she does not. Simone remembers when she and Stephanie, the new girl in school, first met. The new girl's voice enticed Linda. It was full of pink bubble gum and exuberance. These days it emits the slightly rancid scent of roses at the tail end of their bloom.

"We both have to deal with this, Stephanie. I can't predict what will happen. You were Linda's best friend. That means something. Not just to you. Maybe later, sometime in Simone's future, we'll find a way to meet again."

"Do you hear yourself? 'Maybe in the future we'll find a way to meet again?'" Stephanie is furious. "You've got to be kidding!"

She jumps up, water dripping, and leaves without even having her massage.

"Rejection hurts." The thin woman states the obvious.

Wet footprints of Stephanie's departure are mopped away.

The narrative no longer includes her.

Canaries, on the other hand, remain. Simone intends to take over that department of the pet store. Since the theft of the German roller, management has been unwilling to restock the songbirds after they're sold. Simone persuades them that it was a fluke, a crime of opportunity by a lonely old woman or a pathetic vagabond longing for a voice.

"I know what that's like," she tells them. "It won't happen again."

She's busy studying different breeds. There will be a canary orchestra, she promises Sam, with a repertoire of dozens of individual songs.

"Imagine how many people's lives we can brighten!"

She plans a tour of rest homes and hospitals, juvenile facilities. She'll record the performances. She'll have a website. She'll download canary solos gratis to anyone who questions whether it's possible to have a unique, non-replicable voice. "Yes," she will tell them. "And here is proof."

Sam prefers the puppies, and for his birthday, she gives him a hypoallergenic Labradoodle, which he can keep with him even when he stays at Daniel's.

Daniel and the surfer-lady drift apart. She returns to Australia. No longer is Daniel frightened by Simone. In fact, he enjoys her outspoken company. Simone discovers that playing tennis with an ex-husband and Sam, whose nickname 'Squid' has stuck, is more fun than she'd anticipated. The thwack of the ball feels solid and real. She looks forward to the running, stopping, reaching, rallying of the game, and embraces the delineation of sides — fiercely defended—indicated by a mere net, and the simplicity of what is inside and what's out-of-bounds marked by white painted lines. She eases into Daniel's good humor, his joshing with Sam, his generosity at giving her a third chance when she flubs a serve.

Who would have thought that tennis could provide the opportunity for love to regenerate? It takes time, but Simone tires of being a 'guy magnet' and appreciates Daniel's appreciation of her. They start with dinner. At a new restaurant neither has been to before. A first date that's not a first date.

"Uh, do you still like what you used to like?" asks Daniel, looking at the menu.

Simone shakes her head. "It's strange. My taste buds changed."

She doesn't say anything more.

"But you still have an appetite?"

"Voracious." After a moment, "I don't like stews or frittatas or smoothies the way I used to. I want each food item to be itself, not part of a mixture." She looks at him, conscious how much more familiar he is to her than she is to him. "Kind of like how little kids insist on everything on their plate being separate."

"You can taste its essence?" Not quite a question.

"Hear its note," she adds.

"Just so long as it isn't a high C."

He's joking. He's relaxed enough with her to joke.

They try vacations together, and weekends.

Daniel abandons the Time's list of best novels. "Lists are arbitrary. They just appear to make sense," he tells her. "To make it seem like there is progress, a goal to finish. That's not how novels work."

"Or us," she adds.

"Or us." He takes in her sparkling eyes, the short haircut, the gypsy earrings. "It's not how we work, either."

Sex happens. The playing field has changed. There is no routine, or old habits, or expected reactions. Simone excites Daniel. And his excitement arouses her. They find each other anew. Though she keeps her place and Daniel, his, though Sam continues to go back and forth, they are together more than not, and Sam, even without the symbol of a thin gold wedding ring on his mother's finger, feels protected by the circle of family.

Simone has no problem with voice. Not only can she cheer Sam on during his soccer games, she has no problem writing. While she doesn't consider this miraculous, she is amazed at the confidence with which she is able to pen page after page.

"More amazing," she tells Sam, who cocks his head. "I could stop if want. I have a voice. And it is expressed in how I live my life."

"You'll still tell me stories?" He asks.

"Of course."

She makes a final appointment with Dr. Raven who she hasn't seen since that day in the hospital.

# 47. The final session

"I owe Linda one last session," Simone explains when she arrives, a few minutes late, unapologetic, a long crimson scarf trailing behind.

The therapist — no longer her therapist — has trouble following the logic. "Is this like what Prince did? When he became a symbol?"

"Simone's not a symbol. It's a name. It's the name I should have called myself from the start."

Faith frowns. If Linda had been Simone from the beginning, there might not have been a reason for the therapy, they might never have met, and Faith Raven would not have seen the swirl of colors choking Linda's throat, and therefore would not have published results of their sessions in VOICE ISSUES, a case history, which has become a big success in psychoanalytic circles. Faith is invited to speak at conferences, frequently as the keynote speaker.

Simone chooses to sit on the ottoman rather than the floral upholstered chair she used as Linda. The crimson scarf around her neck is a visual exclamation point, reminding Dr. Raven that she is not who she was.

She tells her about Linda's experience in Death Valley, and the transforming power of having intercourse with the sun. She does not mention the stranger.

Faith, amazed at her former patient's gonzo approach to therapy, interprets it as part of a Jungian dialogue Linda was having with herself.

"I was infused with light," is how Simone describes the event.

As she does, she feels a bit nostalgic for the name she used to be. The white skin once circled by the wedding ring has become as tan as the rest of her hand, but occasionally her thumb rubs against the underside of her finger, feeling for the missing band. Unlike her tumor, she experiences its absence. She does not pass judgment on the difference.

Faith nods, but at a certain point in the recitation, no longer pays attention to the details of Linda's Jungian experience in Death Valley. She is listening to the quality of Simone's voice. It is easy, clear, like golden honey pouring out of her throat. This observation is included the next time she's asked to speak at a conference, a finishing flourish that induces nods of satisfaction in her rapt audience.

Finally, she asks, "If you had called yourself Simone from the start, would your story truly have been different?"

A pause.

It stretches and stretches as Simone rewrites the story in her head, over 50,000 words shifting and rearranging. Before the pause extends into silence, real silence, we hear a new sound, one we have not heard before, not on any of these pages.

Simone laughs out loud.

"What do you think, Dr. Raven? Honestly! What do you think?"

And she laughs again, draping the crimson scarf around her neck as she stands up and walks out.

## 48. The Beginning

Simone sits down in front of her computer. She sits down, fingers striking keys.

Chapter One.

Linda's Voice.